STOKER'S SHADOW

Stoker's Shadow

A Novel

PAUL BUTLER

Paul Butler

Flanker Press Ltd.
St. John's, Newfoundland
2003

National Library of Canada Cataloguing in Publication

Butler, Paul, 1964-
    Stoker's shadow : a novel / Paul Butler.

ISBN 1-894463-32-3

    1. Stoker, Bram, 1847-1912--Family--Fiction. 2. Stoker, Bram, 1847-1912--Fiction. I. Title.

PS8553.U735S76 2003   C813'.6   C2003-904532-3

Printed in Canada

Cover design by Trivium

Flanker Press Ltd.
P.O. Box 2522, Station C
St. John's, Newfoundland A1C 6K1
Toll Free: 1-866-739-4420
Telephone: (709) 739-4477
Fax: (709) 739-4420

E-mail: info@flankerpress.com
www.flankerpress.com

For Violet Butler

CHAPTER I

William watches the girl as she silently hangs up his coat; he watches her gold hair catch the muted rays in the lobby, sparkling like tiny flames viewed through a waterfall. "It's rather wonderful," he thinks. "Wonderful and unlikely the way that glimpse of colour shakes the hundred years' dust from my chest; the way it conjures the image of the young man I never quite was."

The boulder has been levered from the tomb for just an instant; a dazzling halo of sunlight has been allowed to escape. And it is a mad, outrageous sunlight which has been let loose in the cavern of his imagination; it is the golden beam which is the source of all life. There are swallows, hummingbirds, and dragonflies dancing in those briefly glimpsed rays. There are mythic flying creatures too, names and phrases caught in his fleeting childhood that have retained a distant thread to his heart. He has just felt the "light-winged dryad of the trees" tug inside him with spirit wings, taking him back to the time of legends when everything seemed in balance.

THE MAID TURNS. She sees him staring at her. But he doesn't feel caught. Her look is open and curious, not afraid. This is part of her charm. She doesn't understand the rules, of course, she isn't English; so how could she know they were both breaking them?

"Is she in the morning room, Mary?" William asks.

He does not take his eyes from her.

"Yes, Mr. Stoker. Waiting for you," she answers. To William, her west Irish accent bends syllables almost beyond recognition while at the same time remaining as light as a stream. She seems to blush slightly; this pleases him too because he loves the way her skin reflects her golden hair.

William shuffles through the little vestibule to meet his mother. The boulder returns and the dust resettles. He opens the door into the verdant jungle morning room. The paradox strikes him immediately. This place ought to be cheerful with its fantastic greenery and its constant pulse of life. But it isn't. There is a funerary air in the thwarted daylight, in the few rays that struggle past the palms and yuccas pressing against the windows. These narrow shafts catch the hanging dust, making William think of the slit windows of a medieval castle.

As usual, his mother is pretending she hasn't noticed him enter. William feels his pulse quickening.

His mother's intelligent pale blue eyes are steady; her gaze rests on a pamphlet in front of her. Her neat, classical features are, as always, a picture of composure – a Greek goddess grown into a wise old woman.

William clears his throat, trying to gain her attention without speaking and legitimizing her pretense. The only acknowledgement, however, is from his mother's parrot which shuffles on the perch and tips its head at William – a faithful centurion guarding its empress. His mother remains quite motionless.

William is unable to take it anymore.

"Well," he booms suddenly, surprised at himself. "How are you, Mother?"

His mother's brow furrows. She raises her head and gives him a benign smile.

"William, how nice to see you! How's Maud?" She turns the pamphlet over.

William clenches his teeth.

"It's nice to see you too, Mother," he blusters. "Maud is very well. What can I do for you?"

"My dear, just by coming to see me you are already doing so much for me."

She smiles sweetly again.

"Well, of course I'm always delighted to come and see you, Mother. But I was wondering particularly why you called me at work this morning, delighted though I always am to drop in on you on the way home."

"What do you think of my companion?"

She gives him a mischievous smile.

William looks at the parrot.

"No, *Mary.*"

"Companion? I thought you took her on as a maid."

"Oh, no, no." His mother lays the pamphlet aside and raises herself from her seat. "She's not exactly a maid."

"If she's not exactly a maid, why is she dressed like one? And why is she answering your door?"

His mother picks up a dainty porcelain spray can and drifts away towards the plants. "She's helping Mrs. Davis," she says. Little clouds of vapour appear between them.

William wonders what traps she is setting for him behind the white puffs and splaying leaves.

He feels his chest tighten. "Helping your housekeeper," he says. He knows he is raising his voice but can't seem to help it.

"My dear William, please sit down," his mother says, reappearing from the greenery with her spray can. "Don't be angry with me. I take whatever companionship and help that is offered me." She gives him a sweet, helpless smile as she returns to her chair. "And in return I can help her take a step up in society."

"She won't take a step up in society by cleaning your floors and answering your door."

But William obeys. He circles the room to the oriental chair near the window. The parrot croaks a territorial warning as he sits.

"We will just have to see how the arrangement turns out, William. She is from Ireland. I may be of help to her."

"Of course," he agrees in order to shut the conversation off. "I'm sure you're right, Mother."

William puts his hands on his knees and gives her a tight smile. "In any case, Mother, what is this emergency you told me about on the telephone? What can I do for you?"

His mother's gaze slips onto the pamphlet now face down on the lacquered side table. "Oh William, I'm almost afraid to show you." But she reaches out and draws it towards her lap. There is a tense silence. From where William sits, he can see the illustration on the pamphlet, a grotesque, crooked shadow, like the cover of a lurid novel, except in the stylized distorted manner of a latter-day Van Gogh. William wonders what such a thing could possibly have to do with his mother or himself.

After what seems like an age, she lifts the pamphlet up and passes it to him. The parrot scrapes on its perch over William's head.

Face to face with the bizarre illustration, he remains none the wiser. The illustration seems to have spilled over from somebody's nightmare. The central figure is neither substance nor shadow, more a mixture of both. Its headlamp eyes and pointed teeth convey a truly remarkable malignity.

And then, in the bottom right-hand corner of the picture, something catches his eye – some German words and then his late father's name: "Bram Stoker." William feels his mother's expectations; he can hear her soft breathing as he gazes. The parrot squawks. William notices the banner of flying rats spell the word, *Nosferatu*. He remembers the word from reading his father's novel when he was a young man.

"Nosferatu," William says bewildered. "*Eine Symphonie des Grauens*." William lets the meaning fall, remembering a few terms of German from his distant school days. "'A symphony of horrors,' of course. A motion picture of father's novel! Well?"

He hands the pamphlet back to her, vaguely aware of an oncoming storm, dimly noticing the strange silence which, from long experience, he recognizes as a harbinger of his mother's withering disappointment in him.

There is a pause.

"Well. I see," says his mother, gripping her chair arm with one hand and letting the pamphlet drop on her lap. "It doesn't seem to worry you, after all."

"Should it?"

"I don't know, William. I'm not sure. Foreigners have just stolen your father's literary property, turning it into an obscene penny-dreadful. Certainly your father wouldn't have stood for it. But maybe I'm old-fashioned." William notices her breathing. It is becoming heavy and rhythmic, her Boadicea-before-battle mood. Suddenly he is desperate to cut this off.

"Ah, ah!" he says quickly. "Royalties! Of course you should have been informed and you must be owed some money."

"Money is the least of it."

"I hardly see that, Mother. There is a lot of money in moving pictures. Much more than you will find in a lifetime of novels."

"That's not my concern. This is your father's work, his reputation."

William smiles. "My father's reputation hardly rests on a free adaptation of one of his novels by a motion picture company. It doesn't even have the same title as Father's novel."

His mother's pupils contract to pinpricks. She fastens William with her stare. "Does it not worry you what people will think?" she asks.

William sighs, defeated. "Not particularly, no. Should it?"

"William, I don't understand you sometimes."

William suddenly feels as though lead weights have been tied to his arms and legs. "I'm sure I must try your patience grievously, Mother," he says.

She stares at him for another few moments.

"Your father was an upright, literary man, not the kind of author represented here." She picks up the pamphlet and waves it in the air.

William sighs. "Mother," he says, "if people in London see this film they won't think anything about Father. Cinema audiences don't think. They'll have forgotten everything about the picture within twenty-four hours and will be running out to see Charlie Chaplin or Douglas Fairbanks. However, I'd be glad to seek advice about the money. I shall go to the Society of Authors."

"If that's the only point you can grasp, William, it will have to do."

A FEW MOMENTS later, William is leaving. He feels as though every ounce of his energy has been drained, leaving him as dry and withered as a museum mummy. He still manages a smile at the young girl. With her rustling white apron now blurred through his tired eyes, she has the quality of a ghost, receding into his dreamworld. She is backing off also smiling, too polite, the sweet creature, to turn her back on him while she withdraws towards the lobby to fetch his coat. He inhales her scent of starch and soap and watches her hands caress her cotton apron; his eyes follow that movement as though he were a snake being charmed.

"I'm sorry. I should have taken your hat," she says suddenly, and William realizes for the first time that he has had it in his hands all this time.

"That's quite all right," he replies. "I prefer informality, don't you?"

She disappears at last, emerging again with his coat. She holds it out and he turns and feels the warmth of her fingers through his collar as his coat rim descends onto his shoulders. She comes a little too close and William feels the delicate prickles of her hair on his neck.

"It's all new to me," she says almost intimately. William feels a sweet tingle somewhere inside him. "Everything here," she whispers.

He turns around to face her.

"It's a lovely feeling, when things are new," he says, smiling. "I hope you make the most of it."

William gazes at the girl's face for another second, her pale skin with hints of pink and gold freckles; again he feels an Eden-like closeness without sin or shame. He smiles at her warmly, then leaves.

ON THE WAY home, William takes a detour. He finds himself by the Embankment gazing at the opaque waters of the Thames. Only the shrill hoot of an omnibus penetrates the relative quiet here. But all sounds are receding. The river holds

William in a spell, the sinking sun glittering on its dark surface. He thinks of his mother's demands. It is as though she is tying knots for him to unpick, drawing him in by using her declining powers as a magnet. William remembers how his father had once jumped into the river in an attempt to save a man. It made the papers at the time. He had risked his own life, the article said. William was an infant then but he had later read the accounts.

William stops walking, turns and gazes towards a small wooden pier jutting out. The sun passes under a cloud. The gold disappears, leaving only ripples of green and black upon the river surface. William can conceive of one reason only why a man would jump into the Thames.

WILLIAM WATCHES THE rhythmic, burrowing motion of Maud's needlepoint. The clock ticks, regulating his thoughts into a more tranquil version of his earlier gloom. Maud looks up at him unexpectedly. He feels caught, as though she can dip into his thoughts.

"Every time you go to see your mother you come home looking absolutely drained," she says.

William shifts in his chair. Maud continues working, her brow furrowed.

"What is it exactly that she wants from you this time?"

"I'm really not at all sure what she wants," he says, then pauses. "What I agreed to was to go to the Society of Authors on her behalf to see what can be done."

"Why?" Maud doesn't look up and continues work.

"Why what?" William asks.

"Why did you agree to something that makes you so uncomfortable?"

William is silent for a long time, feeling the squeeze of wife and mother like shifting mountains, one on either side.

"Because she's my mother," he says after too long a pause.

"Don't you think she is more than capable of looking after herself?" Maud asks quietly, unpicking a mistake.

"No, I don't."

"Oh?"

William gets up with an effort and walks towards the fire. He picks up a poker and begins to jab at the coals. He continues with his back to his wife.

"She's losing something, a sense of judgment. She has someone new, the girl I told you about; neither maid, nor companion, a mixture of both. Sweet girl, but my mother doesn't know what she's doing with her."

William looks around. He can feel his face burning; he supposes it's because of the fire.

CHAPTER II

A breeze whispers hushed-voiced through the white cotton. Mary turns her head from her tiny dressing table, too excited to write any more letters. Instead, she stands, walks towards the window, and tugs the little curtains apart on their brass rollers. She gazes into the star-pinned night and its cobalt sky which falls beyond like a silken cloak. The curtains continue rippling against her fingers like butterfly wings as she draws in the London air. The tingle of the whole Empire dances on her tongue; the perfumes ministered to Scheherazade in her Arabian jail are interlaced with the petal-tongued blooms and burning spices of India.

Her eyes close involuntarily; she can hear the faraway squeal of a tram and the faint whoosh of a motor car. A smile comes to her face unbidden. She feels that she is everywhere and nowhere all at once: she is in the heart of the mightiest city on earth with its proud landscape of stone; she is on the rolling shores of her home in Galway Bay with the rush and sizzle of the tide beneath her feet; she is in an imaginary world of howling wolves and castles, and carriages that hurtle like bullets through the darkness.

SHE KNOWS IT is the novel which lies face down on her dressing table that has excited her, colouring everything with joyful adventure.

She thinks of the letter she has just written, the inadequacy of words. She thinks of her sister, Anne, back in Galway town. She wonders how married life is treating her. Anne will have servants of her own, Mary thinks, now she is part of a merchant family. Her sister's marriage has had a profound effect on them all. Her mother now lives in comfort with her daughter's family. Her young brother, Patrick, will be the first one to go to a proper school, with uniforms and dormitories, receiving systematically the learning for which her family has always had to scavenge, devouring whatever time-yellowed pages they could find.

Books and – at their mother's insistence – books in English had always been their gold. And how right her mother had been! Anne has slipped into a family of standing in Galway because of her well-read English tongue. Indeed, the Callahans see Anne as a rare prize, or as Anne's new father-in-law, puts it "a pearl in the darkest and most unpromising of waters."

The Callahans eased the whole family from the cracked wharves of Spiddal to Galway town itself, the very heart of the Bay. And, for Mary, they went further, arranging with friends for her to find service at the very heart of it all – London.

Now gold was almost free for them all. The Callahans have shelves upon shelves of books and London has a thousand libraries. And more wonderful than that, the lady to whom she is companion is the widow of a famous author. It is too incredible, she thinks, that London could be so rich with literary figures.

Mary closes her eyes again and pictures an invisible conduit between herself and Anne, a magic thread woven from starlight, which might carry her thoughts in more texture and detail than by ink and paper. She replays a scene she enacted earlier in the day. Mr. Stoker's face is again looking at hers, not at a servant's face; at *her* face; like she was a person with intelligence and feeling; like they were connected. "The son of a famous author" she had called him in her letter to Anne. Yet it was not living vicariously at all, though this was how it sounded on paper. Those were just the words, and words could reduce magic to the dullest, leaden tones.

Electricity cannot be explained in words, she thinks. The substance of her heart and soul cannot be reduced to facts and times, especially when that substance touches another. She feels through the scene again slowly. His scent wafts upon her again, a gorgeous sweet smell of tobacco. She captures the good-natured nervousness, not just hers, but his too. She sees his face, rather a kind face, not old but a little careworn with his soft grey eyes. But of all things, it was in the silence that the connection was made, in the absence of bustle – no coughs; no sighs. Stillness and silence; a pool of connectedness.

And then she thinks of her treasure: the book *Dracula* that has been weaving a spell in her; absorbing her old world;

merging it with the new; teasing her inside out with its adventures parallel to her own.

She thinks of the young hero, Jonathan Harker, and of his journey into the towering mountains of Transylvania to meet the Count. Was her own voyage to London not a parallel to that of the English solicitor, albeit in an inverted form? Was she not also a foreigner in a strange land, engulfed by a towering maze of spires and domes – as much of a wilderness to her as the cliffs and peaks surrounding the young Englishman? Was she not surrounded by queer customs and manners, by nobility and titles which she cannot begin to organize?

When she reads of Harker's carriage snaking along the winding road towards the Borgo Pass, the description, for Mary, is interspersed with the black prison-like walls of London hurtling ceaselessly beyond the dusty shield of her train window. As Harker arrives at the black, forbidding castle – a figure alone in a land of the imagination – Mary again beholds the vast, engulfing station with its cathedral ceiling and swooping pigeons. As superstitious villagers cross themselves and exclaim in foreign tongues, Mary's ears are again assaulted by the garbled words of porters and cab drivers.

This city is the wilderness, she thinks; a thrilling, fascinating jungle of stone.

Mary thinks of Mr. William Stoker again. She realizes that, while she was reading and picturing Jonathan Harker's mannerisms and facial expressions, she was in fact seeing *him*. More impertinent still, the feelings of the hero mirror her own so closely, she feels it has been *her* adventure all along as well. She wonders at the fusion between herself and Mr. William Stoker brought about by imagination and a story. She wonders at the strange new empathy she is feeling.

She turns back towards her small dressing table, suddenly dissatisfied with the layout of her room. Thoughts quicken like electricity. She realizes what is wrong. That dressing table and chair should be placed in front of the window so she can overlook the night and breathe in the last blossoms of the season.

FLORENCE STOKER GAZES at the framed pencil portrait of the beautiful young woman which stands on her dressing table – a simple drawing of herself done in profile thirty years ago. She sees the white pool in the eye, the light that represents her soul. She scans over the knowing upward curl of the lip, a humourous, optimistic half-smile; a Mona Lisa touch most impressive in such a limiting format, she thinks. Did she really seem so intriguing to an artist?

She holds the frame in her left hand and runs her right palm an inch over the glass surface, as though it is a genie's lamp with the power to turn some, as yet, obscure wish into reality. She feels as though the image of the portrait must have imprisoned her soul.

A noise somewhere above her room distracts her – a scuffing and scraping from the servants' quarters, as though furniture is being moved. Why would Mrs. Davis be shifting things around at this time of night? She places her portrait back on the surface of the dressing table and takes up her hairbrush. The edges of her mouth, she sees, are turned down in haglike misery. Not a trace of humour or optimism there, she thinks. She knows, in reality, she has not aged badly. She knows she is still admired for her looks. Yet she is unhappy with the image staring back at her tonight.

She thinks over her day, the grey shambling stranger who called claiming to be her son. She remembers how William was as a little child. She sees him standing on tiptoe on the balcony, pointing to the ships' masts and calling out their trades. "Spices, Mama, from India," the piping voice called; "rugs from Persia, Mama look!" That was the William she had called upon for help, not the morose, middle-aged man who smelled of old tobacco.

She thinks of the German pirates who have taken her husband's novel. She sees that dreadful illustration again. Ghastly thing! She thinks of the Lyceum Theatre and closes her eyes. The fragrance of French perfumes and eau de cologne wafts upon her. She remembers how it felt to be at the centre of it all. She sees herself holding onto Bram's strong arm at a premiere. She sees newspaper men twittering around her husband with their pencils and notebooks, begging for a quote from Sir Henry. No one would have dared to try and cheat them then. A great wave of pride rises and crashes within her, leaving in its wake a thousand conflicting streams of sadness. "Long gone," the phrase whispers over and over like foam sizzling into nothing.

Florence presses her palm onto the canvas-bound book on the corner of her dressing table. She has not yet started to read *The Moonstone*, although she had Mary borrow it from the library three days ago. She's not even quite sure why she wanted it, having read it before. Perhaps she wants to submerge herself in the reliable, happy era it represents, she thinks, now that everything around her is creaking with grey malevolence and comfortless subversion. Florence remembers *The Moonstone* as an emblem, not a story. She remembers the Lyceum tour of America, the time she accompanied Bram. She recalls the detour to Niagara Falls, the silver, crystal waters and the exhilaration. She remembers the feeling of the moment; that her life was the centre of everything: past, present, future; east, west, north and south. Bram was acting manager of the Lyceum. He was Sir Henry Irving's right-hand man. The Lyceum and Irving were conquering North America as they had already conquered England.

Florence touches the cover of *The Moonstone* again, as though it were itself a precious gem. Dust from the cover rises with a fragrance she knows but can't place. The room darkens, a murmur of conversation flowing in from some dark nowhere. Stars appear in the shadows of the mirror and just as soon turn into sharp tongues of candle flame. Florence lets herself settle into the recollection as though riding a wave. She sees the Lyceum's leading lady, Ellen Terry, her shining, humourous eyes just above the bobbing yellow flame.

"A Wilkie Collins story!" Ellen exclaims. "That's what the Lyceum needs."

The soft gold light reflects upon the silken green of the actress's dress. Ellen's expression glistens with good-natured poise. Bram is there also, his romantic grey eyes a well of mournful energy. Henry Irving seems to hover over them all, hawklike and saturnine, with black hair and dark eyes. Next to him is Thornley, Bram's older brother: solid, mild and respectable with his round face and white hair.

"Oh indeed," Florence feels herself saying. "Something mysterious but not sinister. Something like *The Moonstone* or *The Woman in White*."

"Unfortunately, Mr. Collins is dead," snaps Irving, still carrying the intense malevolence of Mephistopheles, his latest triumph. The great actor absorbs his parts until they take him over, Florence thinks – a pity he can't play someone more pleasant for a change.

Irving takes a puff of his cigar which he then holds in front of his face like a shield as the smoke rises.

"Are you suggesting that respectability in mystery fiction has died with him?" Bram asks gently.

"I am."

"Indeed," agrees Bram, looking from face to face, drawing them all in, with the steady rhythm of learned oration. "We live in a world of the unspeakable brought to life. Ibsen and the barbarian hordes of 'progress' are beating down the doors of decorum in drama."

"What of the supernatural, Bram?" asks Ellen. "That is where the public hunger is now, surely. Aren't you working on something of that nature yourself?"

"Ah that! I would rather call it 'the unknown.' The word 'supernatural' implies impossibility."

Florence finds herself exclaiming in unison with Ellen. Thornley guffaws. "A mystery, Bram? Tell us."

"The novel I am planning," Bram continues, his audience now spellbound, "is one that penetrates the uncharted territories of the mind, our dreams and nightmares."

"It sounds *very* modern, Bram," says Ellen, beaming.

"Indeed it is."

"Perhaps the Lyceum should follow suit, Irving," Ellen continues. "Perhaps we should look to our own for a change."

Florence suddenly burns with self-consciousness – Ellen has unknowingly activated a volcano in her.

"What are you suggesting?" Irving asks her calmly.

Florence fidgets with the stem of her glass, unable to look up.

"What I'm suggesting is this," Ellen answers, determined to make her point. "That rather than constantly hiring outside hacks to adapt popular stories for major productions, we should use something our own Bram wrote."

Florence shoots a glance at Bram, her lip trembling. She sees his face redden and his huge shoulders hunch over.

"My dear," Irving answers, taking a casual puff of his cigar, "I did not realize you were joining our management team."

Florence dabs her napkin over her mouth, wanting to scream. *Do something, Bram! Stick up for yourself, somehow!* But she knows he won't, and she is just as ashamed of herself for allowing any woman but her lobby his cause.

"Is it such a bad idea?" Ellen says, leaning towards Irving. The two actors are becoming insulated from their surroundings like a married couple arguing.

"I have endeavoured to make the Lyceum the very jewel of our profession," says Irving, leaning back in his chair. "It must never be tarnished by untried hands no matter how well-meaning or industrious their owner, no matter how much affection we have for him."

"Mr. Irving is right," says Bram.

"Bram!" hisses Florence. Suddenly she doesn't even care who hears. A fire of betrayal smoulders in her chest.

"No, my dear," Bram continues in his soft deep voice. "I am still bound in the shallow and treacherous waters of prose. Only when I have mastered that form will I consider turning my hand to the peculiar demands of the stage."

"Bravo!" cries Irving with a clap.

Florence can feel her skin burn like coal. Then an instinct forces her to glance at the door. There, at the entrance to the dining room, is her son, William. He is in formal school clothes, evidently just returned from his school in Winchester. He has grown so much in the last two months that she has to think for a moment before she's certain it's him. He looks like a near-replica rather than the real thing – larger, thinner and darker.

"William!" she cries, reconciling the emotions of joy with worry about what he might have just witnessed.

She flies to the door. "You're home for the holidays!"

The redundant exclamation draws attention to the awkwardness of the moment. Florence hears cutlery clink behind her and she thinks she can see a broody darkness in the boy's eye as she swoops down and takes his head into her shoulder. His bashful resistance seems stronger and more wiry than she remembers it. She tells herself it is her imagination. Boys don't notice awkward scenes. They are too busy with sports and adventure.

She pulls herself away to look at him; tears spill into her eyes. Bram has risen formally and puts out a genial hand which the boy takes looking to the floor.

"How long have you been standing there?" Florence blurts.

"Why?" William replies, looking up. He holds her steady with his grey eyes.

Now she knows for sure; he has seen the submissiveness of his father and it has disturbed him. This boy, half a stranger to her now, has peered into the imperfection of their lives. The poison of reproach and self-criticism is upon them. In some inexplicable way, she feels this is the beginning of a decline.

THE DINING ROOM fades into a landscape of tired skin and shadowed lines; Florence faces her sixty-three-year-old self in the mirror again. Some agent from the other side of the world is trying to unearth all her griefs. And she feels as though she is already upon a precipice. Her own clan has long since passed, or its few surviving members are, like herself, diminished by age. She is the whimpering remnant of an army. She is a relic in an Egyptian exhibition, her bones and withered skin exposed to a leering audience and the flashes of cameras. Something has been set in motion to bring about her last defeat – that German film with its reduced vision of her husband's work; that girl from Ireland. "Was that a mistake?" she wonders. "Should I have found someone from Dublin?" This girl seems too confident. There is an almost presumptuous quality in her open, rustic face with its freckles and in the way she answers questions without the hint of trepidation.

Somehow such optimism doesn't seem entirely decent. It is as though the girl expects she can be at the centre of things. Florence knows these feelings fall short of the rational. And yet something in the house does feel alien since she came. She needs familiarity around her now and she feels as though colonies of strange insects are gnawing away at the foundations of her house, turning the values of her generation into swirling dust.

MARY KNOWS IT'S gone twelve o'clock but she can't go to bed. She just sits at the dressing table which now stands directly below the window. Occasionally, she skims passages from *Dracula*, and the descriptions merge into the night so that the words take form, becoming at one with the breeze which teases the curtain and lifts the pages. Jonathan Harker has been asleep on the floor of a room in the castle, and three strange white-faced women – two dark, one fair – whisper over him, discussing who will kiss him first. The young man pretends to sleep and has a "wicked burning desire" to feel their lips upon his neck. The passage is written in a light, hypnotic rhythm and Mary now more than ever sees the young man as Mr. Stoker. With a warm, bittersweet sensation, Mary also recognizes that she has put herself into the position of the fair woman who swoops down and holds her lips just above his neck until Dracula himself bursts in to stop her.

Mary looks into the night, both afraid of and excited at the fluid, rushing feeling inside her and how she will describe its meaning once it settles into words. The sprinkle of stars is more intense than earlier. She believes she can make out the plough, the same shape she has seen on the far side of her own country. She listens to the silence and slowly a noise forms from the blood rushing in her ears. A glorious, exhilarating sound like claps of thunder, except they are evenly paced and rhythmical – perhaps more like hooves galloping. She closes her eyes and lets the sensation take her over. She opens herself to the night.

CHAPTER III

The carriage rocks. The night is like crystal, silver wavelets shimmering near and far. Huge, bright stars radiate spokes in six and eight directions at once. It is like an illustration from a fairy tale, William thinks. But the carriage sways and jolts so violently, he is afraid that if it is an illustration, he will slide off the page.

William is a child again. The huge leather seat almost swallows him and he has to look upwards to see his mother's youthful face. He feels a little sick, the carriage is plunging so hard in every direction at once. He makes a moaning sound and his mother shushes him gently.

"Where's Father?" William tries to shout. He finds his voice is reduced to a piping shriek. "Why doesn't he save us?"

"He's too busy, William," his mother replies. She hasn't denied they need saving. This worries William. "He's arranging a tour for Sir Henry. When he's finished he'll get us out of this."

As though responding to William's fears, the carriage jumps crazily twice in succession and he begins to hear the ocean like thunder; mighty, earth-shattering, with a thousand whizzing and whirring noises overlaying a deep, ever-changing growl of unrest. William feels that the carriage is a pinprick in hell. Then he notices that two huge sea horses are out in front pulling it along. He sees their exotically curved heads and tails and their rough skin, like embossed leather. The ocean hurls a spray over their heads, a cold dribble sinking into William's hair and oozing its way down his cheek and into the corner of his mouth. The saltiness makes him cough and William begins to see waves rising around him like small shining hills, groaning resonantly as they move.

"I'm frightened," William whines.

"Don't worry, William," his mother replies. "Your father is writing this scene. He wouldn't hurt us."

The carriage sways and jolts, turning on its axis, unsure of its direction for a moment, then recovers.

"You mean we're part of a story, Mother?" William asks, comforted despite the increasing ferocity of the ocean.

"Isn't it exciting?" she says with feeling. "You should be proud of your father."

"I am, Mother; I am proud of Father, honestly." He shouts above the tumult. "What is this story about?"

"We are going to meet Count Dracula's carriage at the Borgo Pass," she says, bending into his ear. "This is why it's so thrilling. It's an adventure – a fairy tale."

"I love adventure!" William says.

But his excitement is swallowed by fear again. The waves are suddenly peaking a hundred feet high, some falling as quickly as they rise, some holding up like misshapen oaks. The carriage is losing its bearings, turning blindly once or twice, then swirling like a cork above a whirlpool.

"Hold on!" his mother shouts.

William closes his eyes, sick with horror. Salt water scoots up his nose and into his mouth; his body is dragged and pulled in many directions at once, like a rag doll being quartered, sheer terror jangling through his body and mind – a train whistle a thousand times amplified ...

... EVERYTHING IS DARK. A cymbal is crashing somewhere in his chest, reverberating through his head and body, shooting hot blood up his limbs. His arms and legs are still swaying, ducking down and rising up; he cannot distinguish one part of himself from another. He begins to hear the sound of his breathing. He can't be under water; he has escaped somehow. There is someone beside him; who is it? This is not a beach or an island. The waves have turned into sheets beneath him. Slowly he remembers his other life, the one that exists beyond the swirling storm. It returns in a patchwork – fragmentary, jigsaw details come together slowly. The woman is Maud, his wife, he remembers.

At this borderline moment, it seems ludicrous that what he has experienced will be described as a "dream" and dismissed as unimportant in a few hours. Yet he knows this is what will happen. It is happening already.

He closes his eyes and waits for his heart to calm. Hammer blows soften to a wooden door banging in the wind, which calms in turn to a dull drumming.

He looks over at the window. Pale light floods into the room. It is a full moon; he can see its perfect rim burning pale blue through the curtains which move gently in the breeze. His bedroom carries something over from the dream: the riches of night and the magic of late summer. Perhaps dreams draw in the flavour of their surroundings by osmosis. This season is like the defiant last stand of summer, the waning nights of faery revelry, when magic and imagination hold sway.

Just for a second, he sees the shadow of wings silhouetted near the pane.

William turns around in the bed, putting his feet onto the floor, checking his balance, making sure his head is no longer swaying. Once he is certain, he glances around at the outline of his wife. She is motionless. He can hear her slow breathing. He stands up and walks steadily to the window. He peels back a small section of the curtain and peers at the garden under moonlight. He sees the mature oak and cedar, the cloistering laurel bushes, and the heavy brick walls surrounding the garden. The outlines are distinct under the generous moonlight; only the colours have been replaced by a generic blue-grey. There is no sign of bird life. It must have been a swallow under the eaves, he thinks. He is about to turn back when he sees that there is a large man with a bowler hat and thick beard standing at the far end of the garden, unquestionably within its boundaries. He is quite alone, motionless, looking, apparently, *at* the house; his features are too obscured by the glass to tell this for certain. William wonders if he should alert the police. But it is a half-hearted impulse held back by several things. Firstly, the man is merely standing in the open, inviting discovery, not hiding or rushing under cover towards the house. Secondly, the stranger's dress is undoubtedly respectable, not the disguise of a thief. But mostly it's the nagging perception that – through the glass, in the moonlight, from a distance – the man *looks* like his dead father.

William turns away for a moment, not exactly afraid, but trying to judge the implications of this last reason. He feels a rising pool of disquiet in his chest, and an odd little hammering sensation returns to his ears. Maud, still sleeping, moans. William peers through the window once more. The man has gone; only trees and bushes sway lightly in the breeze.

CHAPTER IV

William strikes a match, but the damp air claims it, choking the flame. He strikes another, shielding it this time from the wind, then takes a draw and exhales a white funnel into the street's grey canyon.

A middle-aged couple stop on the curb opposite; with their flapping map and umbrella they look like lost crows. Something about the woman – the dark fur of her collar and the hint of comfort it bestows – makes him think of Maud. A boulder turns within William's chest at the thought of his wife – a great rock of sadness, affection and escape, irreconcilable movements pulling everywhere and nowhere.

William continues around the corner. In another moment, the wrought iron statue of Henry Irving appears. Cool rain drips down his collar as he watches the gaunt features of the actor take shape in black. Footsteps clatter around the little square; the dampness amplifies everything. William stops in front of the black rail and looks up. The sculptor could not have known Irving. There is a dignity of bearing, an authenticity about the figure that William never saw in Irving's living flesh. If only Queen Victoria had not had the poor judgment to knight him.

"Sir Henry Irving," the comic phrase rises like hot flame within him. Sir!

A couple of young bohemians – an actor and actress, William guesses – are reading the plaque. They have admiring, fawnlike eyes. How dark his own must look.

Without warning, a breeze stirs and a hundred pigeons feeding at the statue base take wing. They expand in a semicircle around Irving, forming a garland banner. It is as though they have obeyed some gesture from the lifeless monument.

MR. THRING SITS on an embossed leather chair. His desk is heavy oak. A telephone perches at the edge, a large folder splayed in the centre. With his dark suit, spectacles and bald head, Mr. Thring is at one with the furnishings. William wonders if he is folded up at five o'clock and lodged into a sliding drawer in one of the room's panels.

But Mr. Thring brightens when he sees William and he seems suddenly more human. He stands up and shakes hands warmly, then gestures William to a chair.

"I understand you are here on behalf of your mother, Mr. Stoker," he says, settling down again behind the desk.

"That's right, Mr. Thring."

"Let me offer you a cigar," Mr. Thring says unexpectedly, smiling again and opening a wooden case.

"Um, no thank you," William says.

William's head is aching from the previous night and he can feel sore pink rims around his eyelids. He is self-conscious, knowing this haggard look must be noticeable.

"Well let's get to business," Mr. Thring says smiling sweetly again. "We understand and we acknowledge that there is a breach of copyright issue, Mr. Stoker. You can rest assured the Society of Authors will do everything that is reasonably within its scope to help your mother."

William weighs the words carefully, wondering what they mean in practical terms. "Well," he asks after a pause, "what are the options?"

"That's really up to your mother, Mr. Stoker," Mr. Thring replies tapping his pencil on the desk.

"I don't understand."

"We need instructions."

"Instructions?"

There is a silence.

"The question, you see, is this." The words emit from Mr. Thring, soft and quiet, like bubbles in a spring. His gentleness unnerves William.

"How does your mother want to proceed? Does she want payment from the film company or does she want an injunction against further performance?" Mr. Thring's dark eyes twinkle.

"Oh. I see," William replies carefully. "I don't think we've quite decided the question."

"Well, that's what we must know before we hand the matter to our continental lawyer."

William can feel another battle rising; he knows that he may have to persuade his mother not to throw away the chance of royalties.

"I'll have to ask her."

Mr. Thring smiles and rings a bell on his desk.

"Now, Mr. Stoker. I must tell you I am an admirer of your late father's work. The whole subject brings the magic of my childhood wafting back to me." He smiles sentimentally.

William feels the rims of his eyelids burn. "Me too," he croaks.

A young woman enters in answer to the bell.

"Will you join me in some tea, Mr. Stoker? I do so long to reminisce with the son of one of the most frightening men of my youth."

William feels the boulder shift unhappily in his chest, but he tries to relax.

He spends the next forty minutes listening to Mr. Thring's memories of the Lyceum's golden age: Irving playing Hamlet; Irving playing Shylock; Irving's curtain calls; the magical performance as Matthias on the night of Edward's coronation; Irving as Napoleon; Irving as the Vicar of Wakefield; Irving as Mephistopheles.

Slowly, William feels himself becoming twelve years old again. He clenches his jaw, and feels the growing glint in his eye. A black pool of masochism rises within him, and he begins chipping in details that Mr. Thring has forgotten, correcting dates, reminding him of names of supporting players. And then, finally, the conversation slips from the great man to William's father. Mr. Thring remembers the "superstitious whirlpool" of the Carpathian Mountains as described in *Dracula*. He remembers how the characters in the story, once infected by the vampire, become mediumistic, their thoughts and dreams merging. "Such a fantastic idea!" Mr. Thring exclaims. And then he adds quite sincerely: "Your father's imagination must have benefitted so much from being with such an inspired artist."

At first William does not understand. "An inspired artist?"

"Sir Henry."

William looks at the Secretary in disbelief. His round face, bald head and glasses make him seem, for a moment, like a comic goblin. William tries to keep his composure, riding waves of anger and frustration. A few moments later he is gone, pleading lateness for an appointment. He wanders back to his office, passing the black statue of Irving on the way, barely resisting an urge to spit.

MARY ENTERS, FEELING slightly nervous.

As usual, the old lady does not look up although she knows Mary is there – a mannerism that confused the girl for the first two weeks of her stay. Instead, Mrs. Stoker places a bookmark carefully between the pages of *The Moonstone*. Then she looks down in a studied fashion, apparently thinking.

"Mary," she says suddenly.

"Yes, Mrs. Stoker."

Now she looks up.

"Mrs. Davis has informed me that you have moved your chair and dressing table so that they face an open window."

Mrs. Stoker's gaze remains on her as though expecting a reply.

"Yes Ma'am," Mary eventually says.

"This may not be a total evil in itself during the day when the outside is brighter than your room ... do you follow me?"

Mary thinks she has missed something. She goes back over the sentence trying to find it, getting agitated. "I'm sure I need not continue," adds Mrs. Stoker after a pause.

And that appears to be it. Mrs. Stoker's gaze is still on her but there is something resigned and conclusive about it, as though she is about to let her eyes drop to her book again.

"I'm afraid I'm lost, Ma'am," Mary says.

Florence sighs. "Yes, my dear, indeed you are. This is not the place from whence you came, Mary. This is London. There are certain delicacies to consider, certain precautions to maintain." Now Mrs. Stoker seems tired and Mary starts to feel guilty at her obtuseness. Florence fingers her book. "Let me warn you of something, Mary. It is very fashionable these days to question the advice of your elders, to believe that the young have something new and better with which to replace the old order. But you must remember that rules came into existence not through some whim or a wish to keep anyone down. Order and custom exist for a very good reason. The wisdom of ages is found in the most commonplace of rules which it is now so fashionable to deride."

Mary thinks for a moment. *Does Mrs. Stoker think I am trying to deride her?* she wonders.

Then it seems Mrs. Stoker must have read the confusion on her face; she sighs and lowers her voice. "In the evening,

Mary, with your bedroom light on, you can be seen from the outside."

"From the back garden?" Mary says, believing that Mrs. Stoker has simply made a mistake about the geography of her house.

"Precisely," Mrs. Stoker answers to her surprise.

"But there is no one there Ma'am; just a wall and trees."

"If it is dark how can you possibly know there is no one there?"

There is a silence. Mary wants to humour the old lady. "I hadn't thought of that Mrs. Stoker," she merely blurts, half ashamed of her lie.

"Now," Mrs. Stoker says, looking more cheerful. "How are you enjoying London?"

"I love it," Mary responds quickly.

"We must make more of an effort to get out. In the meantime," Mrs. Stoker continues, "did you get a book for yourself at the library? You must not neglect your mind."

Mary immediately colours. "Yes Ma'am," she says overtaken with shyness; she does not know why she can't tell Mrs. Stoker what she is reading, but the information is stuck as surely as liquid in a sealed bottle.

"I hope it is something respectable," Mrs. Stoker responds, perhaps sensing something in her reaction.

"Oh yes, Mrs. Stoker." She almost says the title, but again halts – ashamed of stopping, ashamed she did not tell her before, and now ashamed she has created an unnecessary secret.

"Well I suppose it's all very new to you," the old lady responds.

Mary feels a sting, a fire on her cheek and then a sinking feeling. Mrs. Stoker thinks she is unlearned, she suddenly realizes. Blinking hard, she pushes down her pride to get past the moment.

"Yes Ma'am," she says meekly, "it is."

THE BREEZE STIRS in the afternoon sending flocks of birds spiralling into migration routes. A storm is brewing – a mass of living grey sliding and swelling above the city's spires and domes. Leaves and waste paper dance scattering circles in the gutters. Through his office window, William watches their frantic movements. Then he drags himself into a standing position. He has no appointments and needs to update his mother.

THE WIND RIPS like giant's breath though Florence's garden, thieving plump green leaves long before their withering time, hectoring them in zigzags around the indignant lawn. Florence likes the wind and settles down with the book on her chest. A storm is action; the promise of change in this weary, spirit-deflating age into which her life's journey has had the misfortune to stretch. It is the old order reasserting itself, scorning the 1920s with its grey mediocrity and its grumbling for equality.

Florence closes her eyes and feels the gentle burn on the inner side of her lids – tiredness due to reading. A luminous pattern – green, gold and turquoise like a peacock's feather – greets her from the darkness. The arrangement grows to shimmer all over the wall she is facing. Gaslight lanterns flicker in claret glass holders. The sound of voices, faint at first, grows in substance to a happy, familiar clamour. Expectation floats and sparkles like champagne bubbles, and Bram stands tall like a young oak by her side.

Florence is in the inner lobby of the Lyceum. The brightness of it, the beautiful walls, the perfumes of the ladies and black raven sheen of the men in their evening dress returns to her like the taste of favourite wine sliding over her tongue. She and Bram are at the top of the side stairs looking down, watching each group enter. They nod discreetly as people catch their eyes. Florence can feel the warmth of Bram's forearm over hers.

"Perhaps Mr. Gladstone won't turn up," Florence finds herself saying.

"Don't worry, Florrie," Bram says in his gentle, rounded voice, full of soft vibrations. "The Prime Minister won't miss Irving's *Shylock*. But he must make his entrance when everyone is here to see."

Florence is overjoyed to feel and hear her husband again. She had a terrible nightmare lasting years, it seems, in which she was a loveless, bitter old woman living alone in Belgravia. It seemed so real but is now utterly dispelled by the warmth and familiarity surrounding her.

She is surprised, but not worried, when she looks down at her dress and sees it has changed into a loose-leaf overlapping pattern: part muslin, part silk, after the fashion of the faery queen in *A Midsummer Night's Dream*. "Let's go outside," she says, afraid her attire might seem immodest. "I want to see the carriages arrive."

Bram smiles and they float down the stairs and through the entrance doors.

But as Florence crosses the threshold, something happens. The brightness dims. It is colder. Suddenly, Florence is alone, and not outside the porticoed entrance of the Lyceum, not surrounded by the stone facades of The Strand, but rather in a thick, mature wooded area with overhanging blossoms and forest flowers in full bloom.

As Florence walks, sunlight blinks at her, blocked and released by trunks and branches. This is gorgeous too, she thinks, but she wants her husband and she wants the Lyceum.

"What happened?" she cries out, surprised by how lonely her voice sounds. "Bram, where are you?"

A male voice answers from nowhere.

"He had to leave. He's with Sir Henry."

Florence is a little relieved that someone knows where he is, although she does not recognize the speaker.

The light keeps blinking at her as she makes her way through the woods, touching ferns and grasses with her bare ankles.

"What am I doing here?" she asks.

"You're holding the fort," the voice answers.

Florence thinks of *Dracula*. "What fort? Against whom?" she asks. "Is it a battle scene?"

Florence snags the bottom of her dress. She frees herself with a tug that rips the material.

"This is one of your husband's stories," the voice says. "You're on your own. You must hold them all back."

An owl hoots and some other creature scurries around close to her feet. Florence snags her sleeve. Without warning, the forest dims into twilight.

"Hold who back?" Florence demands.

"Anarchists. The Empire is in danger."

Deep blue darkens to navy. It is night.

A low, long howl emanates from somewhere far off. A winged creature shoots from one branch to another above her head. A whiplash movement and hiss is followed by stinging pain on her ankle. Florence screams and falls to her knees, holding the skin where she has been bitten.

"Bram!" she cries missing his warm protectiveness. "Where are you?"

"What's the matter?" replies the unknown voice that she now begins to dislike.

"I've been bitten by a snake."

"Don't worry. It's in the script."

"I want my husband!" cries Florence.

"Don't you remember?" the voice replies neutrally. "He's dead."

"No!" shouts Florence. Hot tears spill onto her cheeks as the bright illusion peels away. She rocks backwards and forwards in the darkness, cradling her ankle.

As her rocking dies down, the noise of a vibrating engine emanates from somewhere behind her, its steady rhythm increasing in volume and arching into something primal and hungry. Florence spins around. She sees nothing but blackness through the gauze of cracked bark and sprigs. The noise dies away.

Then she spins around again. A squawk – shrill like a train whistle – has pierced the silence, this time from her other side. And now a face comes into view. The face is youthful, androgynous and white like a Japanese minstrel under footlights. Its lips are luminous scarlet and there is a hideous lack of expression; its stare aims beyond rather than at Florence.

Nothing happens at first. And then a branch close to the white face seems to unfold magically in the darkness as though held on wires. Puppet-like, the face moves closer. And Florence realizes it is not a branch, but a limb of the strange creature before her.

Other limbs – green, brown and irregular – disassociate themselves from the forest and other white faces appear, first two, then four, then six or seven, all with the same hollow stare and shining lips. The faces move toward her as the spider limbs multiply, padding through the darkness with a strange, disjointed tread. Florence whimpers and lies down in the undergrowth, feeling wet leaves seep through her garment. She cannot bear one of the creatures to touch her but knows that each second brings that certainty closer. One of the faces hangs moonlike over her and she cannot help but see its dreadful features. They are a ghastly parody of her new companion, Mary. Another face appears over its shoulder. Its glistening paleness mocks her own son, William. She thinks of calling for help but she realizes it is useless; the very breath of the spider people plays upon her cheek and neck as she closes her eyes.

"Mother, wake up," one of them says. She tries to push the creatures away with her palms, but her hands do not make contact. Slowly her eyes open to a very different reality. The smooth walls of her morning room replace the hollow darkness of the forest. Mary and William stand over her, the latter stooping and looking concerned.

"Mother. You're dreaming," William says.

Florence's parrot scrapes on its perch over her head and squawks. The sound is like the train whistle in the forest. Florence focuses hard, collecting her dignity like heavy armour. Reality is still swaying to a standstill and she knows she cannot yet tell truth from dream.

"Mary," Florence says, mustering an instructive tone.

"Yes Ma'am," the girl answers.

"Mail the letters in the hall, will you?"

"Yes Ma'am."

Mary leaves and closes the door behind her. Florence tries to sit up straight in her chair. She touches her cheek with a fingertip to make sure no tears spilled outside her dream. Satisfied, she looks her son in the face.

"So, William. You've come to see me."

"Yes, Mother. I did what you asked me." William is looking at her curiously, and Florence finds herself resenting it.

"What did they say?" she asks.

"They said you have to make a decision."

"What manner of decision?"

William delays answering. Does he enjoy seeing her at a disadvantage?

"Well?" she demands.

William sighs. "A decision about whether you want to try and collect royalties from the Prana film company or whether you want to prevent the film from being shown."

Cruelty rises in her chest like molten iron. "Is that all the progress you have made?" she says.

William pauses and stands up straight. "Yes, Mother," he says with a sigh. "That's all the progress I have made." He turns, crosses to the window and looks out at the lawn. "Sorry I haven't brought you the cheque for back royalties together with a note of apology from the German Chancellor himself."

"There's no need to raise your voice at me, William," Florence replies gently. She finds herself gaining composure from her son's discomfort.

"I do apologize, Mother," he says turning. His face is slightly red. "It has not been an easy day."

"So I see," Florence replies.

William slips onto the oriental chair under the parrot.

"I want to help you in this, Mother, but I need your co-operation." He holds out his hands as though wanting to offer something.

Florence takes a deep breath. "If it's an answer one way or the other that they want," she says looking down, "I want it destroyed."

"I beg your pardon?"

Florence looks at William silently.

"Destroyed?" he repeats at last.

"That's what I said, William."

"The film?"

"Yes."

"Are you sure?"

"Yes."

"May I ask why?"

She finds herself revelling in the moment. She has found an oasis of power. She will splash joyfully in its warm waters.

"No," she says, "You may not."

"No?" he repeats again.

"That's right, William. No."

William smacks his lips and looks to the carpet. She watches him coldly.

"You want me to act on your behalf to throw away the chance of earning possibly large sums of money – "

"That's right."

" – and you won't tell me why?"

"Correct. It is my prerogative and I have decided to guard it."

She grips the chair arm wondering if, after all, she has just dug herself into a corner. This wasn't really a decision so much as an impulse. Her son is staring at her with tired and bewildered eyes. "I would like you to feel the way I do," she finds herself continuing. "That would be nice. But since you clearly do not, I would like to keep my explanations to myself."

"Ah!" William exclaims, smiling rather bitterly, Florence thinks.

"What?" Florence demands. William gets to his feet again and claps his hands together.

"It's a punishment! Of course."

"Don't be absurd!" Florence fires too quickly. She feels her face burning, about to give her away. "Why would I want to punish you?"

William stares back too confidently all of a sudden, almost insolently, in fact. Florence is suddenly afraid of all the answers he could give.

"Because I wasn't as horrified about the existence of this film as you were."

Florence stands. "William," she says, "I am a widow."

Florence turns and walks to the mantelpiece. William has gone silent although she can hear him breathing, thinking. She has just used the mightiest weapon in her whole arsenal and she knows he cannot argue. Florence picks up a display box housing a medal and makes as if to alter its position. The medal is round and silver and nestles in ruffs of silk. It was earned by her husband when he threw himself into the filthy Thames to save some suicidal wretch who, in any case, perished. It was as foolish and dangerous an act as Bram ever performed. But she kept the medal anyway. It symbolizes not only her husband but something about his generation – the full-blooded bravery to which it aspired. She places it back upon the mantelpiece wondering why she has chosen it now. Perhaps she wants her son to see it as a judgment.

Florence turns to William to see him totally wilted. When he answers, it's in a feeble voice.

"Mother, I know you're a widow. That is precisely why you must supplement your situation when a legitimate chance presents itself. Like this film."

"No, William, that is precisely why I have to guard a more precious honour and integrity than mere money."

"How would you not be doing so by claiming royalties?" he asks quietly.

"William, do I really have to explain it to you?"

"Yes, Mother," he replies, "I think you do."

Florence returns to her seat.

"I am too old to join the suffragettes."

"Pardon?"

"I cannot chain myself to a public building when I feel a principle has been violated. My options in life are limited. My powers are curtailed."

William looks at her dubiously for a second but then his head bows.

"But when foreigners distort my husband's words for their own ends, I will use every means I have at my disposal to put an end to their treachery."

William stares at her, pink-faced and unhappy. He nods again.

WITH LEADEN MOVEMENTS, William makes his way to the front door. Mary is already standing there in a plain grey coat and umbrella. She looks down, flicking through several letters in her hand.

He takes in her scents – homely, clean and new – and the grey phantoms of his tiredness disperse almost immediately. "We meet again," he says, managing a smile.

Mary laughs as though he has just delivered the cleverest of quips. Her eyes focus on him conveying limitless trust. She eases on her thin gloves. William opens the door and holds it for Mary who smiles again as she precedes him outdoors.

They walk down his mother's red tiled path hearing their heels clatter through the silence. It is as though the mild flirtatiousness was safe inside his mother's house. Here, without any such canopy, it is more of an effort.

"Looks as though the weather's holding off after all," he says.

"I love it when the clouds groan and threaten for hours."

William smiles at her freshness. They are standing now on the curb outside his mother's home. "Which way are you going?" he asks.

"That way to the post box," Mary answers, pointing.

"I'll walk along with you," William announces casually. "I have to go that way too."

The streets are very empty and quiet and amplify their footsteps.

"So, how are you settling in?" he asks.

"Very well, Mr. Stoker, thank you." She blushes slightly. "I got a book from the library a few days ago. It was your father's book, *Dracula*."

William lets out in involuntary groan, the cloak of last night's phantasm returning – the rolling rocking coach, and the vivid hallucination in the garden.

"Pardon me?" she asks.

"I'm sorry, Mary. That particular book has caused a little trouble recently. What do you think of it?"

"Oh it's so exciting, not at all like the books I normally read."

William nods, wondering what a young uneducated girl would make of his father's turgid prose, thick as it was with cultural information and geographical detail.

"You must find it difficult," he says with sympathy.

"Oh no. Not at all. It's very simple, like a fairy tale."

William slows down, perplexed. "You read a great deal then?"

"Oh yes, I devour books. But *Dracula* is different. Not at all serious."

"Not serious?" William exclaims.

"Not literary, I mean."

He looks at her profile, trying to understand the change. One moment she is a charming, simple rustic from an obscure part of Ireland, the next she is dismissing his father's work as a triviality.

"For goodness' sake, don't tell my mother that!"

"She doesn't know I'm reading it. But I do like it," she adds quickly.

"What do you normally read?"

"I've just finished reading Dickens's *Great Expectations*, and before that *Where Angels Fear to Tread* by E.M. Forster. Do you remember your father writing *Dracula*?"

"Not really," replies William. "He was very secretive and very busy. I just knew he was working on something big." William's mind scans over the dark years of boyhood. An imaginary splash of sea water drips down his face, an echo from last night's dream. Just for an instant, he remembers the shipwreck of his childhood – the event mimicked in his nightmare. He can feel again the dragging motion of the lifeboat beneath him; he sees hands like pig's trotters, pink and swollen, disappear into the black sea beyond the stabbing oar; faces red with mandarin grimaces submerge and rise and submerge again. He remembers his words called through the storm to his unhearing mother: "If Father was here he would save us all!" And then, as though linked by an invisible strand, the fragrance of wood polish and other vaguer perfumes of the theatre whoosh him into a rare childhood moment of privilege and triumph; he has been allowed backstage with his father

whose voice booms like a sea captain through the dark auditorium checking his men are at their posts.

"Mr. Seward!"

"Sir!"

"Mr. Harker!"

"Sir!"

"Mr. Renfield."

"Sir."

Young William loves the pre-performance ritual. It
confirms that his father is a god.

William walks along happily beside Mary, realizing he is
not thinking of *Dracula*, or even of his own cynical late
boyhood years, the era in which it was written.

"How long did it take?" Mary asks further.

"Six or seven years I think."

"Six or seven years!"

William feels stung. He wonders what the girl's amazement might mean considering her judgment of a moment ago.
Does she think it's the sort of novel that could have been
whipped off in a week?

"That wasn't his main career, you know," he replies. "He
was Henry Irving's business manager as well."

"Sir Henry Irving! Yes, I know. He must have been a
great man to know. Maybe that's where your father got his
inspiration!"

Mary looks down as though meditating on greatness.

William sighs, watching her face for a second, feeling a
weight of inevitability on his shoulders. He feels like one of the
conspirators in *Julius Caesar*, boiling with acid cynicism,

fuming at the praise unjustly heaped upon one who is cele-
brated, yet impotent to move even with his white-hot malice
against a man who is already dead.

"And you must have known him too?" she adds looking up
with an open and trusting expression.

Caught in mid-frown, William tries to relax his face. "Oh
yes. I knew him."

Mary has slowed down as they are reaching the post box.
William tips his hat and smiles. "Well, we must talk about this
again, Mary."

Mary's face breaks into a broad smile, dispelling the pride
in William's chest. It isn't her fault, he says to himself, feeling
affection for the girl, for her optimism and innocence. The
same warmth oozes through William's memories.

He walks on alone with the afternoon fog descending
around his shoulders. He is back in last night's dream – the
rocking carriage in vast, crystal night. He replays the vision of
his father through the bedroom window. It's curious how little
this disturbs him, he reflects, considering how very much
awake and sensible he felt at the time.

And as he progresses slowly towards the damp-blurred
lights of the main road, a memory comes to the forefront of his
mind. He is in the Lyceum auditorium again. A fuzzy darkness
sweeps across the rows of empty seats in front of him. The
theatre smell pervades the cool air: the scent of wax polish; the
ghost of perfume from evenings past. William is seventeen and
the magic of childhood and the theatre has long passed. But he
realizes with a prickly nervousness this is a big night for his
father, the eve of *Dracula*'s publication. Bram and the

publisher have been frantically sending notes back and forth for the past few days. His father has been even busier than usual. William – usually shy, morose and distant from his father – has become preoccupied with this, his father's latest venture. He knows there is something special about this book, that it marks a more concentrated, prolonged period of writing than is customary in his father's life. And the result of all the excitement, the event to mark the end of several years of solitary work, is this evening.

Fewer people are present than everyone had hoped. William's mother has not turned up at all, but the young man knows this is just her quirk, her dislike of the macabre subject and her unease with the fact her husband writes it. And there is something slipshod about the presentation. The actors Irving has allowed his father to use from the company are mainly too young and inexperienced for the parts they are reading.

But the main problem is the length of time it is all taking. William's seat is becoming uncomfortable. Dissatisfied noises penetrate the darkness from several areas of the auditorium at once – not the muffled, polite throat clearings of an audience absorbed, but loud, careless coughs and fragments of conversation. This is a "pre-publication reading," not a performance, and with actors merely standing on podiums running through pages of description and dialogue, it is becoming cumbersome.

There is too ample a stretch of time in which to dwell on all the shortcomings: the hurried nature of the makeup; the white dust of fake grey hair on the actor playing Abraham Van Helsing; the anemic vampire with the weak voice declaring with a comic lisp that his revenge will spread over centuries. But worst of all is the contrivance of having so much of the reading go to the vampire-hunting hero, Professor Van Helsing, with the thick, fake Dutch accent and the dialogue his father has written which painstakingly recreates the grammatical mistakes such a character might make.

William squirms in his seat towards the back of the main auditorium. Sweat drips down his spine. "Though we men have much valour and determination with which to protect our so dear charges," Van Helsing drones on, "we must also needs be armed with much knowledge, as knowledge too is a sturdy armour in which we must wrap ourselves. Is it not so, my dear Madam Mina?"

The chatting of the audience has become constant now. There should be a dramatic pause here, but instead there is a steady murmur. "So, I must implore you," continues Van Helsing, a cloud of dust flying off his wig, "what is it that you are trying to tell us, my brave young patient?"

"Only this, professor," Mina replies, looking sincerely into the empty scats and indifferent loungers. "He who has wrought all this great misery upon us all ..."

Someone guffaws. William feels a wire tensing inside him.

"... the very one who has caused this great ordeal ..."

More laughter. William's fists tighten.

"... is the saddest soul of all ..."

Suddenly, voices from behind him rise even more than usual; their tone is excited and conspiratorial. He hears the word "Irving." A hush follows; a hush that has been absent for every moment of the long performance; a hush that is for the benefit of the great actor alone. William knows that Irving is watching somewhere from the back. Hooves begin galloping in William's chest. He wants to rush out of the place altogether. But he is trapped because people will see him and comment on it. So he stays, his heart hammering. He can taste disaster like the air before a storm – tingling, moist and expectant. He knows Irving is going to come up with some "clever" put-down.

Only he doesn't hear it at first. Instead, a sudden eruption of laughter almost drowns the dialogue completely. The seats behind William remain alive with conspiratorial delight, things are being called out from one section of the auditorium to another. "What did he say?" someone calls, and William knows Irving must have left.

"He said ..." the speaker replies through laughter, "'Dreadful!'" The word comes in a rasping, didactic tone, an imitation of Irving.

WILLIAM ENTERS QUIETLY. Ruby, the maid, hovers around him more expertly and less charmingly than Mary, taking his hat and coat. Then he moves into the sitting room where Maud is already reading, one book open in her hand; another, black-bound and anonymous, closed and upon the chair arm. Maud looks at him and smiles.

"What are you reading?" William asks.

"Freud." Maud closes the book. "Freud and *Dracula*. I'm psychoanalyzing your family."

William sits down unhappily. He picks up the newspaper laid on the side table and snaps it open. "And what have you found out?"

"Do you really want to know?"

He peers over the top of the newspaper.

"You want to tell me."

"Listen to this."

She puts the Freud book down and picks up the black book, the back of which has *Dracula* in faded gilt lettering.

Maud clears her throat and unconsciously checks the fastening of her hair. She looks at William with a hint of trepidation and begins the passage of the novel in which Jonathan Harker is asleep on the castle floor and three lascivious women appear out of nowhere to prey on him. William feels his face sting with heat at the strangeness of it. *Why would anyone go to sleep on the floor of an old castle anyway?* he finds himself thinking. He feels exposed and naked as he prepares to defend his father's skill.

But another sensation quickly takes over. As Maud rhythmically makes her way through the description, peering up at him as she pauses, William feels as though a new nightmare is being unravelled within him. A nightmare of troubling, contradictory passions which are at once familiar and forgotten, long-buried in the deep earth of his memory.

Jonathan Harker feels *wicked, burning desire,* that one of the women will kiss him and at the same time a *sickening dread.* He waits with a *languorous ecstasy* when he smells blood on their lips. But at the very height of this teasing expectation, Count Dracula bursts into the room ordering the women away and claiming the hero for himself.

At this point, Maud stops and looks at William.

"So," William asks, afraid but defiant. "And what does that tell you?"

"I don't know," Maud says, her brow furrowing.

William feels his body stiffen. He puts his hand over his mouth pretending to check for stubble.

"But, if my husband wrote that," continues Maud uncertainly, "and if I was twenty-five years older, your mother's age, with rather more old-fashioned views, I think I might feel threatened by it."

"She never seemed threatened by it to me."

"Maybe not in the past, she didn't. But she's threatened by it now, isn't she? She's threatened by what we'll make of it today in 1922 with our greater liberty to discuss matters once hidden."

"I hardly think so," says William, deflecting the darkness which looms from Maud's suggestion. "People of my mother's generation were hardly innocent. What about *Dorian Gray*? *Dracula* comes practically on its heels."

"But *Dorian Gray* talked of perversion while *Dracula* kept it all hidden and encoded."

"I don't think there's anything hidden or encoded about it," William insists, wondering at this lie and feeling his face burn again as he repeats it. "It's a simple, straightforward story about vampirism."

"I don't think it is about vampirism. I think it's about something else."

"Naturally," William responds. "You've been reading Freud."

"Do you ever think about Henry Irving?"

William shakes his head impatiently.

"I mean," continues Maud, "about what his influence on the novel might have been?"

"The only influence he might have had is lead actor if *Dracula* was ever turned into a stage production." William begins to scan the paper again but immediately his imagination is overtaken by a matching of pictures so vivid and intense it cannot be denied: the pigeons whirling around Irving's statue meld into the pamphlet illustration of the German film, the thin, crooked vampire and the banner garland of flying rats obeying their master.

"Why are you so sure about that?"

"Sure about what?"

"You made up your mind that the answer was 'no' before I even asked the full question."

"I don't understand you," William says frowning, lowering the newspaper again.

"You don't want to talk about Irving and his influence on your father. It's a painful subject for you."

"Nonsense," William insists. "I was talking in great detail about Irving to Mary, my mother's new girl."

"You talked to the *maid* about Irving?" Maud says.

"She did most of the talking." William pretends to be absorbed in a headline. "And she's not a maid, I told you. More of a companion."

"Well, whoever she is, she's lucky to get you to talk about something personal without prising it out of you the way I have to."

William drops the paper onto his lap. "Firstly, it wasn't a personal conversation, it was small-talk. Secondly, I felt sorry for the girl at the beck and call of my mother. And lastly and most importantly, I was walking down the same street at the same time so my options were either to talk to the girl or ignore her, pretending not to know who she was. I'm sure that's the course of which my mother would have approved. I'm rather surprised to find you agreeing with her on such matters."

William is breathless and overheated after this diatribe. He snaps the paper up again, but has to put it down as his wife responds.

"Those were your only two options, were they, William?"

"Yes."

Feigning confidence, William begins to look at the paper again.

"Sometimes I wonder. You talk about your *mother's* judgment failing. I'm not so sure she's the only one."

"What is the matter with you, Maud?"

"I'm sorry," Maud sighs. "I just find it hurtful when you can be so carefree, so natural with some people, yet so brittle when you're with me."

"Maud, I can assure you I have not been 'carefree', as you put it, with anyone in the last little while." He suddenly feels tender towards her and speaks gently. "You are not missing out on anything. I am quite miserable all the time."

Quite suddenly, Maud relaxes and laughs affectionately.

Ruby enters with a tea tray.

William and Maud become silent.

CHAPTER V

Mary drowses, watching the curtains ripple and flutter, caressed by unseen hands, drawn silently through to the other side and returned just as gently into the room. She lies in the room's darkest corner beneath a sheet and a single blanket. The moon radiates like a bright half-halo through the little open square. Blue light skims off the window ledge and touches the tip of the bedpost at her toe.

Mary follows the dovelike movement of the curtains, carried along by the gorgeous fantasies in Dracula, *and the heady, succulent images of blood and death. One passage is replaying in her mind: Jonathan Harker peering out of a castle window at night only to see the Count slowly crawl like a lizard down the sheer vertical wall, his cloak spreading around him like great black wings. She thinks of the disbelief that must accompany such a sight, and the abandon it must take to weave such ideas into a story. She looks into the soft, magical darkness and thinks of Mr. William Stoker.*

WILLIAM IS FLOATING *on the undulating breeze. He does not quite recognize the garden around him which abounds with midsummer life: squirrels, rabbits, swifts and swallows darting from tree to tree. But the bright starlight and the intoxicating scent of wild roses seem to echo a world from his childhood, a mythic forest of paradise and plenty which seems to have been always beyond the rim of his imagination. He wafts effortlessly past the grand cedar tree with its levels of luscious green from which heads and tails of squirrels appear and disappear as though lost in the ecstasy of endless discovery. Although the moon is out, there is sunlight too. Day and night interchange constantly like brightness and shadow beneath a half-clouded sky. Patches of the garden dance joyfully in pools of gold, just as others glisten in the silver-blue of night. Each is the equal in beauty to the other; in both moonlight and sunlight every blade and leaf dances with the impossible, glorious happiness of perpetual life and motion.*

A pale brick wall comes into view with ivy trailing upwards like a river. William follows spirit-like, inhaling the white ivy blossom as he reaches it. He finds his outstretched hand is touching the cool moist stone, and slowly his hands and feet join onto the wall and brush against the ivy leaves and branches as he begins to ascend. His fingers ease effortlessly into the wall as though it were putty and he feels a sweet sensation as if his hands and fingers have gained the ability to taste. A hummingbird whirs at his shoulder and he lifts himself higher, enjoying the sweet moisture from the brick as it seeps into his skin. He raises himself from sunlight into a patch of glistening moonlight and becomes aware of soft ringlets of gold suspended above him. He ascends further and feels the silken joyous texture of golden hair tumbling upon his forehead and cheeks, like delirious, sparkling rain. He caresses the hair with his hands and whispers tenderly the name: "Mary, Mary,"as her face comes into view before him.

A second later things have changed. Mary is in Middle Ages costume again and William is standing in a dungeon with his back against a dripping wall. William looks into her bright smile and ocean-blue eyes. She pulls the black shackles from his hands, letting them drop like licorice. Mary comes closer, her lips so close to his neck that her warm breath touches. "Mary," William murmurs again. Darkness closes around him and he notices that everything has turned to a horizontal position and that the dungeon wall has become soft and hollow, obeying the contours of his back. He calls her name into the darkness once more and then sees the window and dressing table in the indistinct moonlight.

He shoots up in bed, aware suddenly of Maud's warmth beside him. He watches her dark shape closely making sure his wife is asleep.

SHE MAKES A low primal groan which subsides into a slow exhalation. William assumes she must be in a deep sleep. Reassured, he gazes towards the moonlight-brightened curtains and remembers last night's vision. He feels drawn to the impossible, to the idea his dreams are part of a message in cipher, something that will lead him ultimately into the garden of paradise he keeps glimpsing – towards the notion that his father's spirit might be a messenger leading the way, telling him where he took a wrong turn.

Carefully, he pushes the covers off his legs and turns so that his feet touch the rug. Then, shivering from the unexpected chill, he stands and takes a step towards the windows.

"What," Maud moans.

William realizes he has miscalculated; she is waking. He feels trapped.

"What!" she says louder.

"It's ... don't worry, it's just me," he replies, not moving any closer to the window.

"What are you doing?"

"Nothing."

"Are you ill?"

The moonlight catches her bare arm which reaches up to her forehead; her neck is raised from the pillow.

"I'm just going to check the garden," William says, too muddle-headed to think in terms that make any sense.

"Check the garden? You know I'm a light sleeper, William. I wish you wouldn't do this."

"I've never done it before," he replies, comically stranded on the rug, as though unable to continue without permission.

"You did it last night," she replies sighing and banging the pillow behind her. "Why are you checking the garden? What's wrong with it?"

"There's a man standing in the middle of it."

"What?" she replies laying her head down again on the pillow. "You're having a nightmare. Come back to bed."

He sighs, turns and climbs back into bed. He watches the curtains move slightly although the windows are closed.

THE SHINY PALE leaves and knotty clumps of oriental twigs and branches look incongruous to Mary's eyes, especially beneath the sliced fruit cake. But it is as though nothing in England *is* English – at least not the china she has been polishing all morning. In the last hour, she has travelled the globe. She has encountered the curved, bronzed features of Indian princes with loose silken trousers and earrings. She has viewed the snow-ridged mountains of some unknown eastern highlands populated by men with huge furry hats and skinny moustaches. And now finally she is gazing at the sparse, decorous beauty of the Japanese court with single trees, waterfalls and beautiful white-faced women.

"Shall I take the tea in, Mrs. Davis?"

Mrs. Davis glances up as she places the teapot on the tray. She smiles naturally, like one used to pleasing.

"Well yes, Miss Manning, that would be a nice idea."

Mary wonders whether Mrs. Davis is as confused by Mary's status as she is herself. "Miss Manning" seems wrong coming from a lady twenty years older than her. She has always been just Mary in Ireland. And here her elevation makes little sense. She does the chores of a servant most of the time. She lives in the servants' quarters. Yet Mrs. Davis is almost deferential.

Mrs. Davis opens the scullery door and Mary departs holding the tray tight, trying not to let the Japanese china clink so hard it may break.

The tray wobbles as, one-handed, she opens the door. She remembers not to knock – knocking, she was told very early on by Mrs. Davis, is a *faux pas*. (Mary did not know what a *faux pas* was and Mrs. Davis had to explain it to her. From then on the puzzle has been less about strange customs and more about why the English constantly lapse into some foreign dialect when they feel threatened.)

Within, Mrs. Stoker sits with the bald, bespectacled man to whom Mary had answered the door. Mary wants another look at this Mr. Thring who seems like a character from Dickens, all angular details, and delicate, thought-out movements. Neither Mrs. Stoker nor Mr. Thring look up as she enters and places the tea before them on the little mahogany table, but there is a silence and she assumes one of them is about to address her. But no; it's just a lapse in the conversation.

"Well, when your son came to see me yesterday, I realized that if I had any news at all – good or bad – I must take the golden opportunity to visit the famous Mrs. Stoker."

Mary feels stranded between Mr. Thring and Mrs. Stoker, her shoulders beginning to slope as she tries to work out whether she should speak, leave or pour the tea. She is about to ask Mr. Thring whether he takes milk and sugar when Mrs. Stoker answers him.

"I do believe, Mr. Thring, that you are an incorrigible flatterer, but may I say a delightful one." Mary turns to see the bright openness of Mrs. Stoker's pale blue eyes; it seems she has become a different person entirely – younger, happier, almost playful. Then she hears a more familiar offhand whisper saying, "Just leave the tea, Mary, I'll deal with it."

Mary's ears begin to burn only when she gets to the threshold of the sitting room and the hall; only then does she feel the full force of the disparity, the less-than-nothing esteem in which she is held. She catches muted words through the closing door:

Mrs. Stoker: "Poor girl, I hoped that London might have made something of her."

Mr. Thring: "How generous of you to take her in."

Mary faces the closed door and breathes in the foreign scents of wood and wax pervading the hallway. For a moment she hopes they are talking about someone else. After all, the exchange makes little sense with reference to herself – she was in a better social position in her own homeland by far, especially on this evidence. But with a dull thud, she realizes that the unthinkable is true. She is the unnamed "her," the imaginary figure cowering in the gutter. She wanders slowly back into the scullery, towards the little oasis of civility she finds in Mrs. Davis.

The housekeeper's dark, intelligent eyes catch hers for a second as she kneads a wedge of dough. Mary peels off her apron, feeling like a ghost – numb and detached from reality.

"Mrs. Davis, I'm going out for a bit if you don't need me."

Mrs. Davis smiles, her hands still working. "So you should, Miss. Get out and see some sights."

MR. THRING IS conjuring a magic world for Florence – her own past coloured by the admiration of youth. He is describing what she had believed the world to have forgotten – the flamboyant and invincible circle to which she once belonged, characters who could easily have been woven into the great mythic tales: Arthur and his knights, Jason and the Argonauts, Sinbad and his wild voyages in search of riches. He talks of men who leaped through flames, daring all upon principle – Whistler's libel action against a spokesman for the brutish, philistine public and the penury that followed him; poor Oscar's fierce last stand and the even worse fate that came to meet his defiance. But they were men alive with the fire of valour and faith. These things are their own rewards.

"And where are we to find such colour in today's drab world?" says Mr. Thring.

Florence feels the warmth of comradeship in the heartfelt comment, so much so that her sadness spills into words before she can stop them.

"My son, for instance."

"Ah," Mr. Thring notes, not disagreeing.

She wonders at her cruelty but feels a twinge of revenge not so much against the forty-year-old man as against the insolent boy who had once eavesdropped at a dinner party and then answered so sullenly.

"Not like his father," she adds, twisting her hands together.

"Indeed, but what an act to follow, Mrs. Stoker!" He is now defending William, it seems, albeit gently. "What a man to live up to!"

"How true," Mrs. Stoker says quietly, guilt stirring then subsiding. "Author, theatrical manager and barrister-at-law." She plucks out the titles one by one, like trophies. Her favourite is the last – she never really enjoyed his stories, although she was pleased when others said they did – law's respectability and stature speak for themselves.

"I had no idea Mr. Stoker had been called to the bar," Mr. Thring says, impressed.

"Indeed he was, Mr. Thring."

"Did he practice often?"

"No, he didn't actually practice," Mrs. Stoker says, wondering why this always comes up as an issue.

"Not at all?"

"I believe not," confirms Mrs. Stoker taking a sip of tea.

"Goodness! Too busy with Sir Henry, I suppose."

The unhappy thought enters Florence's mind that her husband could indeed have achieved much that was both respected and remunerative if he had not been so tied to Irving. Why had he made life so difficult for himself? It's a dark puzzle she is afraid of unpicking. And there is another piece of business pertaining to Bram's career. Mr. Thring is so charming she has almost forgotten the news he has come to give is not good.

"Now, to get back to this film, Mr. Thring," Florence prompts.

"Of course," he replies.

"I understand that the company – "

" – Prana Films," Mr. Thring nods.

"Quite so ... that has committed this atrocious theft has gone bankrupt and that this may delay punishment and destruction of the film itself."

"Yes," Mr. Thring replies colouring a little. "All the property of Prana Films has been in the hands of the official receiver, it transpires, for some weeks ..."

"And the culprits are free?"

Mr. Thring shifts in his seat. "Prana Films no longer exists as a legal entity. So any claim to damages would have to go through the official receiver."

Florence lays her cup down. "This is most unsettling," she says. "For a theft to take place and then for the perpetrators so simply disappear in a puff of smoke is ..."

"Most unjust, I quite agree," Mr. Thring says firmly.

"And it is not damages I want from them, Mr. Thring," Mrs. Stoker continues, her courage rising. "It is damage I would like to do to them."

"Quite so," Mr. Thring says very seriously.

"When I think what might have happened, and that only providence prevented this thing from coming to London to smear my husband's memory in the open. I must have this film destroyed at the very least."

Mr. Thring lurches forward in his seat. "Unfortunately," he says wringing his hands, "there are probably a number of copies."

"A number!" Florence exclaims. She feels as though her problem has just multiplied like so many fast-breeding insects. "Why would there be more than one?" She hopes he has made a mistake, that he knows nothing about this business.

"It is common practice, I believe, to have many copies of a moving picture so it may show in many cities at one time."

Florence has to prevent herself from rising. The image of this horror spreading like a disease around the world is just intolerable.

"Please don't alarm yourself, Mrs. Stoker," Mr. Thring says calmly, "I'm sure we will find a way. We will be patient and hope for co-operation from the receiver. This is an outrage and we will do all in our power to put it to rights."

Florence looks into Mr. Thring's dark, trustworthy eyes. She begins to breathe more easily.

"Now," he says, looking down at her Persian rug. "There is one last little problem."

The pause makes Florence worry.

"There is a very small 'film society' as they call themselves, here in London." Mr. Thring takes out his handkerchief and dabs his mouth. "They meet somewhere in Knightsbridge, I believe. Only very limited numbers turn up, I'm sure." Florence senses that a dark invasion is about to overtake the green and ordered land of her memory. "They appear to have got themselves a copy and are advertising among their very small membership a presentation of the film tomorrow night."

The invasion has started. The barbarians are overrunning the hills. Florence takes a deep breath. She feels the galloping in her chest and hears herself called to action. She thinks of Bram diving into the murky waters of the Thames, regardless of propeller and undertow. And then she sees it in herself: the shining, swift blade of defiance.

Chapter VI

Silver ridges, like mermaids' fins, rise and fall as the sunlight dances over the water's surface. The weight of his father's hand on his shoulder provides the profoundest comfort to William. Father can make everything right with the world, *he thinks.*

He knows his father can dispel all fear and worry, unpick and untangle every dark chain, lock and puzzle that childhood nightmares can devise. His father is a wise magician, a weaver of tales and an important man who is revered and looked up to. When William is afraid of school, afraid of leaving the certainty and warmth of home for some bleak unknown place, his father tells him stories of valiant knights who go in search of their grail. Then William feels the safety of virtue closing like armour around his chest and shoulders and warming his heart. He knows that the fire of uprightness will burn for him through any desolation.

And here on the balcony of his home overlooking the
Thames, William is in paradise. The constant rippling
sunlight on the water's surface sends eddies of optimism
through his spirit.

"You see this river, my boy?" his father says. That voice
with its curious balance of great strength and gentleness acts
as a balm for William; it tells of mightiness stooping to
nurture; it tells of power all-knowing, all-seeing, all-forgiving.

"You are watching the busiest waterway in the world,"
his father continues, and William peers over the balustrade to
see the white linen-like sails pointing into the rich blue sky,
and the industriously churning wheels of the steamboats.
"You see the schooner with the long white sail?" William
fixes upon the vessel which closes upon a ramshackle
wooden pier, and the men throwing ropes as thick as dungeon
chains upon the board. "That ship is carrying woven silks
from Arabia."

William stares enthralled, wondering why the men do not
look like Sinbad with white turbans and shining trousers. He
looks at the white pinnacle of the vessel's sail and imagines
the sandy peak of one of the great pyramids.

"Those barges by the eastern dock haul a thousand spices
into the heart of our Empire."

William follows his father's pointing finger, settling on
the tied-up vessels bobbing upon the tide below the dark
wood-shuttered warehouses on the south side. His mind
follows his father's weaving descriptions, and he conjures the
most glorious colours of silk and ruby and emerald from the
scattering gold of the sun. "I want you to remember always,

*my boy," his father continues, "that if you are brave, fearless
and forthright in life, you may choose your destiny from the
infinite possibilities you see before you."*

*The promise is overwhelming; the beauty of the world
and his place in it is simply overpowering. William closes his
eyes in ecstasy.*

THE WASTE PAPER dances a little circle in the tiny alcove
courtyard where no sunlight penetrates. William watches,
trying to re-conjure the magic of the memory. He wonders
about last night; whether he would have seen the figure in the
garden once more if he had reached the window before Maud
called out. Maud had forgotten about it, thankfully, by break-
fast. She clearly thought his belief in the watcher was a mere
delusion spilling over from his dreams.

Now that the tide of boyhood memories is flooding over
him, William finds he wants to believe in his father's ghost, or
at least in some faery spirit that may choose to have pity and
rekindle his withered soul. He had always felt that belief in the
supernatural was the last refuge of the desperate, the final
piece of driftwood at which to lunge before sinking finally into
blackness. Now he is prepared to acknowledge his desperation.

William lifts his gaze from the dingy corner with the waste
paper now scraping near the gutter grill. Above, a triangle of
bright sunlight turns the grey stone almost gold. The tiny
courtyard has no apparent purpose and was built entirely
enclosed from any street. Only near midday does sunlight
creep upon the upper reaches of its well-like depth. And the

light here intensifies even further now as though released suddenly by the passing of a wispy cloud. William stands. Called by the cumulation of spirits which have gathered lately to haunt him – his father, his own boyhood, the lavish fantasies of youth – he feels himself drawn away from the office, the accounts that await his attention and all other composite parts of the dreary straitjacket of routine he has fashioned for himself. He sets forth to meet the sun.

MARY FEELS LIKE a convict escaped into paradise. She has broken the shackles and defied authority – *possibly*. The rules which govern her are so vague and changing she isn't even sure whether or not she is allowed to leave on her own impulse. In any case, for the first time since her arrival, no one, except herself, knows where she is and no set tasks and timetables are before her.

And the strangest thing is she can think of nothing more daring to do with her unexpected freedom than to duck into the library and read some of her favourite new book, *Dracula*, which she has brought with her in her cloth bag. For a while the scent of leather and wood, and the library sounds – muted footfalls, soft whispers and the creaking of chair and table as the elderly man opposite her strains to read his text – seem both comforting and appropriate. But soon a feeling less savoury pervades her chest. She reads of Lucy's death and Dr. Van Helsing's plans to save her soul from the torment of living death. She reads of his sharpened stake and his instructions to all the young heroic men who have formed a brotherhood. And somehow it all seems less satisfying to Mary than the earlier part of the story when she followed the young man, Jonathan, on his quest into strange and foreign lands.

The elderly man opposite begins to wheeze and his chest makes crackling noises like a bonfire in the rain. Mary glances up, unsettled, seeing huge saucer eyes magnified through finger-thick lenses. Suddenly, she feels reined in, strangulated by the man's infirmity. She starts resenting the bleakness of her refuge and the ineffectual modesty of her rebellion. Her own chest begins to feel constrained like one of the vampire's victims.

She looks around, wanting to throw off the feeling. Rays of sunlight from the high windows intensify. Mary watches as the bright rays land upon a distant bookshelf. Little spots of gold appear on the faded spines. It is as though the aged gilt lettering is being awoken after a hundred-year sleep. Mary lets a new feeling flood into her. The ground beneath her begins to rumble from an underground train. The floor shakes harder, dust flying off the nearest bookshelf. The old man opposite takes out a handkerchief and wipes his nose.

She is here in London. What will she decide to do? She makes up a list in her mind: Marble Arch, London Bridge, Trafalgar Square, Covent Garden, St Paul's. She remembers her arrival – it seems like years ago now although it is still measured in days. She remembers the swooping pigeons and the vast, ornate station. The infinite promise of that moment comes back to her, asking her the simple question: *"Why not?"*

Mary returns the book to her cloth bag and looks into her tiny leather purse to double-check the presence of two shillings, a threepence, and two pennies – all she has left from her journey. She rises from her seat tingling with both pleasure and fear.

Outside the library, she tries to get her bearings. She is on Ebury Street. If she turns left, and instead of going back to Mrs. Stoker's house, keeps on in the same direction, she will reach Buckingham Palace in less than thirty minutes, then Green Park in another five and then Piccadilly.

She sets off. A breeze sweeps past, playing with her hair, scattering small leaves and brown paper about her feet. The air smells of soot and diesel, mixed with earthy, natural scents. Newspaper vans and omnibuses thunder past, their huge wheels spinning, exhaust pipes coughing out dark smoke.

Soon the streets change, becoming wider, busier and more commercial. As the buildings become loftier and more ornate, with lions' heads, dragons' heads, griffins' talons and angels' wings carved into the stone, she begins to feel light and impervious to fear. Her expectation for unseen hands to reach out from doorways and correct her erring path begins to fizzle away into the sunlight. Maybe Mrs. Stoker won't even notice. Maybe it isn't even against the rules. She is less convinced by this second thought than by the first, but she has counted the cost and taken her risk and now she is enjoying the crime.

Shiny wrought iron spikes to her left herald what Mary knows to be the Buckingham Palace grounds. The young women who pass her now are in the highest of fashion, with loose-fitting dresses, falling necklines, braidless hair and a carefree nymphlike manner. The way they walk is different too – gliding and effortless. Around the square outside the Palace and along the Mall, they float past in groups, linking arms with each other like wild spring flowers turned into necklaces. Or sometimes a young woman will hold onto a dark-suited man, her spindly arms pulling at him possessively – an odd and almost indecent reversal of protector and charge. These creatures revel in the early fall, laughing at the first falling leaves and the hint of pre-decay richness which wafts and billows between Green Park and St. James and along the tree-lined promenade which leads to Admiralty Arch. Mary watches these amazing, confident women; she sees the light touch of a youthful white hand upon a shawl or shoulder fur, an action claiming the luxury of the moment rather than warmth. She is drawn by their confidence. Yet she is dimly aware there are multitudes of greyer people on the street who are less noticeable and more like herself.

Mary continues under the grand porcelain-white arch and into Trafalgar Square with the giant black lions and the towering obelisk. The great commander, Nelson, seems to sail along in the air under the white passing clouds and Mary feels dizzy when she tears her eyes away and looks back down into the square. She sits down on the broad paw of a lion, feeling at one with the crowd from whom shouts and exclamations come without shyness or reserve. The thunderous square with its teeming life and pigeons merge in Mary's mind with the shingle and rock beaches of her home in summer, where children dance circles on the shell-littered shores, dodging gulls and loading buckets and pans with nature's bounty. There, too, the divisions between people seem to dissolve and the group is like one many-headed being, unified by the experience of the magical season. Although she misses Anne and her mother, she feels them in the strangers who absentmindedly press by her shoulders, and she is thrilled that such innocence and joy can be found in the very heart of the famous forbidding city.

The sun becomes stronger as Mary moves away from the lion, her protector. She goes to a stall and buys two postcards from the man in the checkered cap in the newsstand who can't stop talking even between customers. She will write to them both tonight she promises herself, and she will describe how she spent the afternoon. She passes by the National Gallery, thinking she ought to go in, but then decides it would be sacrilege to turn from the sun and the teeming multicoloured life around her. She turns into a quieter lane and then sees a figure in shiny black – the same colour and pattern as the spikes forbidding entry into the Palace grounds.

Then she gasps out loud as she reads the name: *Sir Henry Irving*. Her heart leaps with serendipitous delight.

That the whirlpool of experience around her should suddenly hone into this pinprick of coincidence! She gazes at the austere figure, its thin face, hawklike nose and black, expressionless eyes. Mary thinks of Mr. Stoker's sad, grey eyes and how as a child, and perhaps as a very young man, he must have beheld the flesh and blood version of what now stands before her. That the invisible strands of fate should have woven all these things – the book, Mr. Stoker, Mrs. Stoker and this statue – together all in the space of a few days seems marvellous to Mary. And it sends her mind reeling through time and space, to all the other things in life that had once seemed beyond her touch yet which, in fact, could easily lay before her in this new universe of the possible.

She remembers the crockery from this morning – the wild and exciting representations from all corners of the globe. Images flit before her of the Eastern-looking arcs and buttresses and the exotic swirls in stone that have come before her eyes even in her short walk so far; London it seems to her now, must be centre of the world. She determines to dive even further into its riches.

WILLIAM STARES INTO the jar of spiced whole mangos before him, and feels a curious empathy for the fruit trapped against the preserving glass. He picks it up. Maud appreciates it when her pantry is stocked with unexpected pleasures. She enjoys asking Ruby to put exotic delicacies out on the table with the cold meat. But William is really on a quest of his own; he wants to find symbols of escape in the exotica he knows to be hiding in even the most conservative parts of the city, like here in the Piccadilly shop where the hidden joys of the Empire are collected and sold in neat, colourful packages. He wonders why he should have thought of food, particularly – he has also visited the Twinings tea shop in The Strand and supposes it to be because the scents can escape from the packages, forming invisible wings of fragrance to carry him to the far lands of his imagination.

William's eyes skim away from the whole fruits to the pickled lime with the label decorated with red and yellow Persian designs. He imagines himself just for a second in an Eastern bazaar, his ears assailed by a reedy wind instrument and the frantic shouts of merchants. Fantastic coloured spices pile up on makeshift wooden stalls and trembling scales.

Women of great beauty and dubious reputation await assignations under pillared archways.

With a flush of embarrassment – especially as the features of the first woman he visualizes are a darkened, Eastern-tinged version of Mary's – William catches the eye of a young male server, uniformed in a turquoise waistcoat and breeches. The boy looks away suddenly.

William wonders what his expression was revealing. He gives a business-like cough and takes himself off to another section, the quaintly ancient floor creaking beneath him. He drifts over to the tobacco stall, where his gaze is claimed by long, thin Turkish cigarettes which lie in little pyramid arrangements under glass. There is something pleasingly forbidden about them; their appearance carries an echo of the Eastern-style opium dens of the city now extinct but once the secret playground of his father's class and generation.

A female form draws quite close to his left side. Without looking, he can see she is dressed in a light-grey coat, fastened rather loosely at the waist. If a lady, he thinks, she must be of dowdy disposition. He notices that she is craning her neck to see his face. The sultry bazaar woman wafts back into his mind. And a second later, he finds himself addressed.

"Mr. Stoker!" the young voice says, gasping in surprise. "I knew it was you!"

He spins quickly to see Mary's face, with more colour than usual, animated with surprise and delight.

William finds himself skipping a breath and taking a half-step backward. Her twinkling blue eyes and optimistic smile whirl in a cocktail with the Bacchanalia already surrounding his senses. The lurid shimmering cloak of his desire is suddenly edged with the most exquisite innocence.

"What a coincidence!" she cries, smiling more brightly as though reacting to the surprise in his face.

William feels his cheeks burn but is determined to keep a sense of composure. Mary's straightforwardness is as unsettling as it is charming; he has to struggle against the impropriety of such openness even while he enjoys the warmth from her vivid expression. A frowning ginger-haired counter clerk has appeared behind the tobacco display. William turns from him to address Mary and, in doing so, figuratively takes her arm; they do not touch but a physical understanding causes her movements to coincide with his as though she is a mirror image. They sway away from the clerk attached, like Siamese twins.

"So my mother has set you free for an afternoon," he says, feeling the mention of his parent will absolve him of anything improper. A quick glance behind, however, proves that the clerk's interest has, if anything, grown to full disapproval.

Craving the open, where glances and stares might seem less stifling, William guides Mary down the creaking aisle toward the exit. Mary explains, somewhat awkwardly, that she did not seem to be needed so has come out to see the sights. Not really listening to her, William replaces the mango jar on a shelf as he passes.

They cross the threshold into the sunlit open and William asks her what she has seen. Excited again, Mary names the places she has passed. She becomes especially animated as she talks of the bustling life of Covent Garden and how it made her feel she was in Italy, and how no place in London really felt like England but usually like some other country. As they walk along, William realizes he does not know their destination, or where and when it might be proper for them to part. With an oozing pleasure, he becomes aware that Mary's abandonment is so great the question is not even occurring to her. An idea – a folly of flirtation but harmless enough – passes through his mind; they are coming close to the Ritz Hotel and William has an idea he would like to see this girl lost amidst the extravagant leaves of Palm Court, an excellent place for afternoon tea. He feels light and youthful as he steers her through the wide entrance with the wrought iron gate lodged permanently open. Mary halts in mid-sentence – she was talking about how she feels watched by the griffins and gargoyles that perch upon so many buildings. William registers her soft confusion with a raising of his eyebrow and a smile.

"Where are we going?" she asks, as their footsteps clatter over the shining marble entrance floor.

"Follow me," he replies smiling. "Let's sit down and have some tea."

Mary stares in something between fear and wonder at the many layers of splaying palms, at the crystal ceiling and at the insanely ornate fireplace with golden nymph and cherub statues reaching out in three-dimensional relief, holding cups and swords and bunches of grapes. William coaxes her to sit before one of the Ritz employees, who is dressed like an over-done courtier, has time to pull out her seat. He orders quietly while Mary lets her cloth bag flop by her feet and takes it all in. Then he turns back to watch her clear blue eyes scan the surroundings, not so much like the innocent fawn of poetry as the sentient, critical being he knows her to be. It occurs to him that, rather than being impressed by the luxury, she might actually be horrified by the gaudiness. He waits while she settles, and when she first meets his eye, she smiles with a warm but unspecific enjoyment.

"What do you think?" he asks.

She returns his smile, knowing she is being teased. The expression and the pause that follows are perfectly judged to make William realize that she is not an underling, maid, or young woman in need of help or patronage. She is William's equal, someone who, except for the natural advantages of age, can match him in every respect.

"It's so lavish," she replies at last, "more like a cathedral than a tea room."

"I used to come here when it was first built," William replies with a hint of apology. He realizes he must have been thinking about Maud and their courtship days when he decided to bring Mary here. He must have thought the excitement he once shared in this place could be transferred somehow to the present and to a different coupling. "It was quite the thing once," he says simply, shifting in his chair. "How are you enjoying *Dracula*?"

"Oh, I wanted to talk to you about that!" Mary replies, returning to her fully animated, positive self. "I've had the strongest reactions all the way through this book." She bends over and reaches into her bag, pulling out the battered novel with the faded cover.

"You've brought it with you!"

"I was in the library before I started to explore," she says, blushing again and William wonders why.

She puts it down on her knee and looks at him intently. "I have this feeling ..." she says, rooting him with her ocean-blue eyes. Then she looks down for a second, trying to work out how to say it. "It's like vampirism isn't entirely bad." Mary looks up again and then shakes her head, frustrated that she cannot explain.

William smiles and finds himself glancing around at the other mainly empty tables. The only other customers are a lady with a long feather in her hat that dangles every time she takes a sip of tea, and a demonstrably bored younger companion. They seem to be beyond earshot. He wonders why he should be worried. Perhaps it is Mary's earnestness. There are devils of cynicism carved into the very foundations of this city. Mary cannot begin to imagine how they wait to devour her.

"What I'm trying to say," she continues, "is that something happens to people, to Lucy and Mina, when they fall under the influence of the vampire. It's as though they get mixed up with Dracula, become part of him and he becomes part of them, and then – and this is the strangest thing – it's as if the good characters ... the ones we are on the side of ... become bad."

William looks at her frowning, struggling to understand.

"What I mean is," she continues, "When they – Dr. Van Helsing and the others – go to kill Lucy in her coffin, they become worse than Dracula. At least he doesn't pretend to be good." She sighs, dissatisfied with her explanation.

"I understand what you're saying," says William sincerely. "The villain becomes more sympathetic as the story goes on."

"Yes," she agrees helpfully, still not quite happy.

"Perhaps it's because my father was an Irishman. He had a complicated view of heroes and villains. It's something that happens to those of us from the colonies," he says, looking directly at Mary, indicating that he means her too. "I think we find it difficult to stick to one opinion about good and evil."

"Why?" she asks thoughtfully. "Why would that be?"

"Because our masters are at once our friends and our enemies, depending on how we feel treated." He catches her serious, intelligent gaze and continues. "And in any case, they can never be completely our friends, simply because they are our masters."

Mary continues to look at him searchingly. William finds his cheek burning. "Like my father and Henry Irving," he continues. "To my father, Irving was master, enemy and friend." William notices a strange silence falling around them. His voice is soft but it carries. A clinking cup from the table of the feather-hatted lady alerts him to the fact that people are listening; something in his tone must have told them of a possible impropriety. But William continues to meet Mary's gaze. She is leaning slightly towards him across the table, drawing words from his innermost depths. He is a bottle uncorked, spilling ideas which he was hardly aware of possessing.

"There's a kind of a devotion that runs through the Stoker line," he says. "My grandfather, Abraham, toiled devotedly for the English in Dublin Castle, sacrificing and resenting all the way, passed over for promotion, locked out of the highest social circles because he was too Irish." *How long is it since I have even talked about all this with Maud?*

He seems to float away from himself for a moment and watch himself from another table – a flushed, middle-aged man unburdening himself before a beautiful and intrigued young woman. The intensity of the couple shows they are sharing secrets. The nature of the secrets hardly matters; shared confidence always weaves intimacy.

William knows why the feather-hatted lady and her companion have gone silent. His soft, resonant tones waft the flavour of yearning through the air. The twin subjects of family and devotion have been chosen because, from here, he can unravel his love song, or at least its mournful prelude. William has been here before – to this very place many years ago with Maud, speaking in the same soft, intense tones about similar things, drawing the same warm focus from his companion. *Why am I trying to relive it all now?* he wonders.

But Mary seems fascinated; soft fires show in her irises. William finds he cannot stop. "Anyway, Abraham passed on his disease to my father, although in a different form."

"You mean Irving?" asks Mary.

"Yes. Not the British Empire exactly. But another kind of icon. The prince of the stage."

William is surprised by how romantic his voice sounds and by how much the girl seems under his spell. Yet he feels a hypocrite; however poor his forebears' attempts to escape this family curse, no one's struggle seems as bleak and half-hearted as his own.

"But you don't see yourself as Irish, do you?" she asks, still excited.

"By blood, I'm completely Irish," William replies.

"But Mrs. Stoker – surely she's English."

"No, she's Irish too."

"But her accent, and she seems so ..." Mary doesn't finish but William thinks he understands.

"People of my mother's class and aspirations do not necessarily keep their original tongues," he says with a slight smile. "Has she not told you of her years in Dublin?"

"No. She doesn't speak much, except to ask for things."

The serving girl comes with tea, dainty sandwiches and an assortment of cakes. She places the tray before them without a sound and begins to pour the tea. William and Mary are silent. The serving girl catches William's eye – a hostile look – as she switches the tea spout from one cup to another. William's face burns. But Mary is oblivious, looking around contentedly. The serving girl leaves.

"I hope my mother is paying you fairly," William says hoarsely.

Mary gives a slight cough and withdraws the cup from her lips, putting it down on the saucer.

"We have never talked about that," she says, dabbing her mouth with a serviette and colouring.

"What do you mean you haven't talked about it?" William asks rather too forcefully.

Mary looks up with a hint of pleading in her eyes, as though she'd rather leave the subject alone.

"Nothing really. We've just made no arrangement about that side of things."

The black clouds of impotence suddenly clear from William's mind. The fire of action burns in his heart. Armour tightens around his chest. He hears his father's voice whispering about just crusades and battles found by providence in the most unlikely corners of one's life. Here, at last, is a fair, pale maiden who needs rescuing. Only the perversity is distracting, that he must save her from his own mother.

He shifts in his seat and covers his mouth with his palm. "Explain this to me again, Mary," he begins. "You're telling me my mother has made no provision or specific undertaking to pay you?"

Mary stares back with wide open eyes, the cup handle suspended in one hand.

"Well," she begins, pained, "there has been no mention of it ... and I haven't asked!" She blurts the last part as though defending Mrs. Stoker.

William leans forward and rubs his hands together. "Mary," he says quietly, "if you are acting as a companion to an older lady, in other words as a friend, someone who would attend the same events, meet the same people and be introduced into the same society, it might be acceptable for you not to draw a salary. But this, as I understand it, is not the case. Correct me if I am wrong."

Mary looks defeated and embarrassed. "Well, Mrs. Stoker mentioned something about that. She said we would do things and go to different places."

"But you haven't?"

"Not yet." The words drop like soft clay and her moist gaze rests upon the table.

William suddenly regrets spoiling her tea. He realizes that in his fervour he has been pushing her into one of two imperfect worlds, that of official servant or unpaid friend. He would like her to be a companion so that the growing intimacy between them might continue. But he cannot live with himself if he lets his mother exploit her; it would confirm his own non-rebellion.

"I'm sure we can sort something out," he says softly, already wondering how. Mary manages a weak smile which pleases him. Her trust has not been broken by his juggernaut charge into such forbidden areas as money and status. A thought weaves unbidden into William's brain. *How far might this licence go?*

William smothers the idea quickly with visions of himself as protector. His father's heroes stir within him as he thinks of Mary's defenselessness; he feels the weight of an imaginary scabbard by his side and the steel of armour on his chest. The demons that wait to devour this young woman, he thinks, are subtler than any vampire or rogue. They cower in the hearts of those who claim to protect.

CHAPTER VII

The gorged maggot ceases to move in the apple flesh. All the wind-fallen cherries, bramble-berries, dewberries, plums and crabapples which lay scattered over the greens and parks of the city are slowly changing from within, fizzling in their own yeast, turning to heady wine within circles of mould and bruising. Twilight creatures scurry amongst the undergrowth, their senses altered by their warming, fermenting diet.

The night is calm and silent with a distant promise of frost. Stars burn cold through the deepening blue. The breeze stirs from the north, rattling the driest leaves and circling meditatively high above the rooftops from which the first wisps of smoke begin curling.

William listens to the tick of the mantelpiece clock and hangs onto the ridge of the passing summer. He is aware that a great change is coming within himself, and is half accepting, half frightened of what this might be.

MAUD OPENS THE book and William's resentment of her rises like vinegar in his throat.

"The Thing in the coffin writhed," she quotes calmly, her delivery purposely neutral and non-sarcastic. The effect of such "fairness," William knows, will be to sharpen the blade of damnation when it finally falls onto his father's story.

William tries to stay calm. He has a long bridge to build if he wants to turn the unease he feels into a rational objection, and he knows he is unequal to it. So he retreats into passivity as Maud recites the passage. Her measured tones describe the twists and contortions of the vampire; the vampire is Lucy, friend of the novel's main heroine, Mina. But the narrator, either Jonathan Harker or Dr. Seward – William can't remember, they switch so often – no longer refers to her by name, or in any human terms at all, so intent are the vampire hunters upon her destruction.

William feels as though his wife is similarly torturing him. As the stake is plunged and then hammered into her chest, he feels like screaming out that she is defiling his father's memory, trampling over his grave. But he knows his agitation is ludicrous; she is, after all, merely quoting his father's own story. He fixes his gaze on the ducking flame in the newly lit fireplace, feigning tired indifference and superiority of knowledge as Maud goes on to read about the vampire's lips champing together until her "mouth was smeared with crimson foam." The lurid vulgarity gives him a start which he is at pains to suppress.

At this point Maud coughs a little herself.

When she continues, her voice is hoarse. And new perversity enters the scene. The passage describes the expression of the impaler, Arthur, who is one of the heroes of the novel. Even though Lucy was his own fiancée before her infection, Arthur is "like the figure of Thor," with "high duty" shining in his face as he bears down with all his strength on "the mercy bearing stake." Compounding his weird moral reversal are the prayers of his vampire-hunting circle – four men in all – which begin to ring through the vault, in a ghastly climax of hypocritical piety.

Maud finishes, closing the book slowly and looking at the rug. She looks up and William looks away.

"Well," she says conclusively.

"It's just a story," William sighs.

"Do you find it embarrassing?"

"Why should I?" He gets up and walks over to the fireplace. Then, realizing that to start poking the fire again would be too obvious an obfuscation, he turns and faces his wife with his hands in his waistcoat pockets. "It wasn't supposed to be analyzed, it was supposed to be read."

"Yet both you and your mother are treating it as though it is a landmine sitting in the mud. At least I can't seem to get you to talk about it."

"I don't mind talking about it," William says blushing at the lie, and realizing that he has repeated the exact same behaviour as the day before. He has once again talked almost freely about it with Mary but is clamming up with his wife. "I don't understand what it is that you want from me," he says rather rudely, and immediately regrets it. "I mean," he adds softly, "I don't quite see the purpose."

"Aren't you curious?" asks Maud.

"About what?"

"About what your father thought of women," she pursues quietly. She watches him closely as he leans against the mantelpiece with an elbow.

"He loved women. He adored them."

"He appears to adore Lucy too, until about halfway through this novel of his."

"She turns into a vampire," he says emphatically.

"Very convenient." But she smiles in tired defeat, takes the novel from her lap and places it on the little coffee table in front of her. She takes up her needlepoint.

William returns to his seat. He finds his wife's intrusions unsettling. What right has she, after all, to trespass into his father's mind? He realizes that there is more at stake than this. Her exploration agitates him because, by unpicking the privacy of his memory, she is weaving her way through his own mind as well, not just that of his father. His father is within him, William realizes. He is merely another chapter in the same book.

With heated discomfort, William becomes aware also that his growing infatuation with his mother's new girl is woven into the same secrecy. They are part of the same great vine, protecting the same dark desires. He has not mentioned his tea at the Ritz with Mary, and he is steering away from any talk about his afternoon that could force him to lie. He wishes to delay the moment of confirmation, but he knows the direction in which he is heading. He knows he has already passed the sign marked Danger. And now, as his wife's fingers start their rhythmic movements with the needle, he thinks of the tangle he has created for himself. He has pledged himself to help Mary and the mission now burns urgently in his heart – this is a monster obligation he has been feeding with the abandonment of despair. How, he wonders, can he elevate Mary's position without raising suspicions as to his motivations?

Both mother and wife, it seems, stand in his way. As he already helps his mother with a small allowance, the only way he can lobby in Mary's favour would be to increase that monthly payment. Such an initiative on his part would raise his mother's suspicions. Given her contrary nature, he might not even get her to agree. And it would also involve an open conversation with Maud. Most crucially of all, he knows himself to be quite unpracticed at this kind of subterfuge. He knows the walls he has erected are far too fragile not to be swept away instantly by minds as penetrating as those of Maud and his mother.

William stares at the fire listening to the hollow tick of the mantelpiece clock. Maud, oblivious to him, works dexterously at the needle.

Urgency presses upon William's spirit; this mission to help Mary, dark and imperfect as it is, is part of the great redemption that has been filling his dreams of late, part of the golden chivalry he has been seeking to claim. Even through his wife's reading of Lucy's impalement, another vision ran like a loose thread – that of his mother with the stake and Mary in the coffin. It was upon Mary's breast that he saw the white dint of flesh stand out as the stake point descended. It was Mary's white face that came alive in screaming pain as the blood spurted out through the silver shroud. And in the background, he glimpsed his own form, lost in the shadows behind his father's heroes with their Latin prayer.

The flames die down and the coals begin to glow. William wonders why his urge to save Mary should have to be so utterly soiled. Separate from desire and romantic secrecy there is, after all, an important mission to achieve. Thoughts of self-chastisement begin to deflate William. If only Mary's saviour were a worthier knight, one capable of more selfless dedication. He thinks of his father. And now he remembers an important distinction. It was Lucy's soul the men in *Dracula* were saving, not her life. If he could recall the conversation with his wife, this is the true argument he would pursue. Their standards were so lofty, the codes of chivalry so perfect in their total dedication to the adored one, that they would not allow Lucy to shame herself in death; they would save her from the degradation of the vampire existence that chained her and threatened to mock the purity they knew.

William thinks of his father, and of his absolute dedication to Irving. This was a type of chivalry too. He remembers how his once robust, striding parent was reduced to a bearlike creature bending over his study desk, collating his life's work before that life dripped entirely out of his weary spirit. He remembers how his father's decline could be measured to a point in time as precise as the pivot, and how that point in time matched perfectly with Irving's death in 1905.

And what did his father choose as his great task once the black clouds of mortality began rolling toward him? What great work did he feel compelled to complete? William remembers how the answer had confounded and frustrated the young man he was at the time. Now his father was free to live for himself and spend his time writing novels. But the letters, scraps and old photographs that started to litter his desk were not research for an original story. They were not the cumulation of frustrated dreams now released in a torrent of creative energy. These were the raw materials for another kind of great enterprise. And this all-absorbing task was simply to mirror everything that went before. The turmoil of preparation in his father's study was for a book to be entitled, *Personal Reminiscences of Henry Irving*.

As though he had not dedicated enough of himself to the actor! William thought at the time. He remembers the surprise he felt at his mother of all people, never Irving's greatest admirer. Rather than trying to persuade him towards a more selfish path, as William felt sure she would, she spent many hours a week earnestly filing, searching, scanning materials for this same great work. He remembers how tender she was to her husband in those years, indulging him in all the details and fancies that had once been her daily irritations.

William recognizes now what it was that changed her. For the first time in his life he feels something like it himself. She was in awe of her husband's love for Irving. She had seen the inescapable divinity in a devotion so great that even his own obituary should be a tribute to his friend.

FLORENCE LIES FACING the dark ceiling. She listens to the groan and creak of the windows under the gusting wind. It is a comforting, eternal sound which exists quite beyond the sordid, troubled present. Her soul drifts effortlessly between

pitch blackness and the shining gold of her memory. The loneliness and terror of her later life tumble away like dark leaves
in the wind, turning to joy and sunlight in a second. The darkness returns, but only for a drumbeat before tumbling again
into open blue skies. The ever-changing moan of the wind
holds her in the season of perpetual alteration. She fears
nothing, as nothing lasts beyond the moment.

The warmth of her visit from Mr. Thring established a base
of joy that cannot be entirely eroded by the frustrations that
followed: her foolish, disobedient maid leaving without a word
and returning so late; her own inability to deal with it straightaway; and the constant aching in her arms and legs, a herald
of the trying season to come. But the tingle of starlight is there,
beyond it all, reminding her that, whatever the drudgery that
followed, she had once been on the mountain, surrounded by
gods and legends, and that this is her natural home.
Endurance is to be expected. Downfall is inevitable. The blight
of destruction is already in London, and within the walls of her
house in the presumptuous young woman from Galway Bay
she had the poor judgment to accept.

But all this does not wash away the glories of the past;
glory is transient by its very nature.

Florence's thoughts darken, the leaves turning over into
blackness again. She becomes aware of the dim oil portrait of
her husband in the shadows overlooking her bed. It's curious
that she has grown so used to ignoring it, but that very lately,
she has caught Bram's tired and sombre eye while turning
toward the wall at dawn, or slipping into bed last thing at
night. Bram makes her uneasy. It is as though the ten cold

years that separate their last meeting have done more than time is supposed to do; they have turned them into strangers, perhaps even enemies. That lonely stretch of time has worn away the happy memories. Like wind over sand dunes, each time she has talked over the past with friends, she has unwittingly altered the landscape. She can no longer remember what she actually felt.

And then there is another kind of recollection, the type that remains locked deep in the vaults of her brain, troubling her more with each unwelcome encounter and growing in strength and clarity. These memories are like sea monsters feeding upon silence and fear. And they are pressing upon Florence now, surfacing with a whole range of sensory detail – she can even taste the flavour of the dust – clearly delineating the time, place and mood.

One lasts for just a moment though its sadness and confusion are eternal. She is in the very bed that she now lies upon. But she is gazing off at the window. Her husband's body lowers the bed's opposite side into a valley. But something is wrong. A terrifying noise breaks the silence in staccato rhythm, a kind of gasping, muffled yelping. Jolting movements accompany the sound, shaking the bed and rattling the headboard against the wall. Florence keeps her body stiff, unmoving. The unacceptable horror that her husband should be crying – an action of such unmanly despair from a proud, protective man – is surpassed by the probable cause. She knows that Irving said something cruel about her husband's new novel earlier. A special reading had taken place today and she overheard a remark made by someone who had attended.

Florence listens hard. Could there be any explanation for this dreadful noise? Gripping the pillow with her hand, she tells herself that it is sometimes difficult to tell. In the still of night even snoring can sound like a battalion laying siege with a full arsenal of cannons. She closes her eyes and tries to convince herself her husband might be snoring.

FLORENCE NOW STARES at the ceiling, remembering that night twenty-five years ago, wondering at a man who can be so utterly wounded by words. And why, if it was true? Why was her husband's happiness so tied to the actor's opinion of him? It is the very uncertainty that now alienates her from her dead husband's portrait. And then the leaves of her imagination twirl again, and she wonders if something else is unsettling her. Was she, as wife, not guardian of her husband's happiness? Was her duty not to battle through the fortress of his manhood into his confidence so she could soothe and share his cares? She thinks of Portia and Brutus. Would this noble woman have turned away into the night, listening to her husband's sobs and not acting?

She takes herself off to another time, another sea-monster memory but an antidote to the first.

THIS TIME SHE is hovering around the shadowed hallway, butterflies whirling around her stomach. Arcs of sunlight stream through the semicircular glass above the door, resting upon the bouquets whose fumes add to the cathedral solemnity and ease Florence's agitation. Florence tries to imagine how she will greet her husband when he arrives home. She can hear both the clomp of horse carriage and whizz of motor car engine. Every sound makes her jump a little. "Irving is dead," she tells herself, running her hands down her dress, making sure reality seeps in so that she might better know how to behave in front of Bram. She remembers seeing herself from above – her disembodied spirit watching from the hallway ceiling. She recalls how – in viewing her nervous, guilty flitting from one corner to another to ensure the flowers were visible from the doorway – the reality of it descends on her: her husband has just suffered *the* loss, the one they have both spent their married lifetimes dreading. And everyone else knows it too. In the last twenty-four hours, flowers and letters have been arriving steadily, all addressed to Bram. Florence has fielded inquiries not just from newspapermen, about when Bram is expected to return from Bradford, but from the whole theatrical circle. The death notices cite Irving's estranged wife, but for the Lyceum crowd – for those who actually know them – the real widow is her husband.

Florence remembers the soft light of pain in Bram's eyes in the first weeks of his return and the alteration in his face, a claylike stiffness in the substance of his skin. And she recalls his wan kindness towards her, as though he were suddenly aware of *her* own disappointments, her own second place in his heart. Most of all she remembers the certainty of one feeling, a certainty she accepted quite passively, as she recalls it, that the good years were over.

Florence lets the memory go, soothed by the vision of softness in herself. And something earlier and brighter is about to take its place, a reward perhaps, when a most unwelcome sound emanates from the ceiling – one she did not expect to hear: a determined, scraping noise which seems to start in one part of the room and ends in another.

CHAPTER VIII

The fingers of the breeze pull Mary's hair like a playing, reckless child. The wet gusts moisten her eyelids blurring the vision of the grey-blue clouds rolling over endless spires and rooftops. A long groan emanates from beyond everything. The clouds gather speed, glowering, regrouping and preparing for battle.

Mary feels that her adventure has begun at last. Her tea with Mr. Stoker seemed to confirm the real connection between them. He even flirted with her a little, guiding her into the Ritz Hotel without letting her know. It was sweet really, how he expected her to be impressed by it all – all the jungle palms and the outrageously vulgar statues carved into the fireplace. But this was only half the victory of the day, Mary thinks, feeling the cool rain land in thick dollops upon her cheek and forehead. She took a chance and defied the old lady and her senseless, inconsistent rules. She broke out of her cage and returned when it suited her to find the cage still open and no punishment planned. And now she is claiming her own adventure again, breathing in the night which Mrs. Stoker has tried to forbid to her; she is watching the clouds crawl like living membranes over the city. She is pledging herself to take part in the magic world before her.

THE MORNING SUN floods brightly in from the shining wet garden. Florence makes "shushing" noises into the cage as she pokes the monkey nuts through the thin bars. The sound calms herself, she half realizes; the parrot is indifferent. Florence is thinking of the sea, of Whitby and Cruden Bay and of summer holidays past. It feels as though a mystery has unfolded to her at last; she feels she knows why old people like the sea. It is because it tells of corruption and eternity, of things that are whole breaking up first into pieces, then specks, and then dissolving altogether under the constant roll and tumble. And it tells this story in a manner not altogether uncomforting. The horny claw of her parrot reaches out and takes the husk. It performs the task with infinite care. *How gentle the world is being to me this morning!* Florence thinks. She hears a cough from the door.

"Mrs. Davis?" She calls without turning.

"Yes, Ma'am."

Florence looks around. Her housekeeper is standing just inside the room. "Where's Mary?" she asks.

This is the beginning of her own great enterprise, she tells herself, the one that began forming in the dark and sleepless night. "My own obituary will be one of defiance," she told herself through the relentless memories and tumbling nightmares, "and I will start writing it in action once I awake." She will represent *her* people, *her* tribe, the golden generation now gone that now relies on her, its representative.

"In the scullery, Ma'am. Shall I fetch her?"

"No," Florence replies quickly, picking up another nut from the bowl. "Wait a moment." She has been looking forward to meeting her enemy for hours. But now suddenly she is afraid. *This is one of the ants who had been chomping through the foundations of my house,* she reminds herself. *And I have power over her. I have the power to eradicate this threat.* But she still wants to delay the moment. It is as though the insect might have grown to enormous size when she wasn't looking, developing sharp talons and yard-long steel pincers.

"Last night I heard the shifting of furniture in Mary's room again," she merely says. She drops the nut into the parrot's cage, but the bird refuses to come this time. *Am I really so afraid?* Florence wonders. *Is this an attempt to get Mrs. Davis to reprimand the girl for me?* She thinks back to the interview with Mary a couple of days ago. She remembers the clear, blue eyes of the girl and the disingenuous answers she gave. Sincerity and simplicity can be frightening things, Florence thinks, especially when the message to be conveyed is one of subtlety and nuance. Too much honesty can border on insolence. Florence is remembering her dream and the spider-like creatures unfolding from the forest, how one of them was so much like the girl.

"I expressly told her to leave the furniture where it was," Florence says, turning around at last, and feeling her heart skip a beat. She knows that every word she speaks now is committing herself to something more. She is crossing the border of no return. "I believe you did the same. It seems our message has not got through."

"I can go up and see if you like, Ma'am," Mrs. Davis replies. "Perhaps she only shifted a chair slightly or something." Mrs. Davis turns to leave. Florence stops her, sensing an alliance.

"No," she says calmly, "I shall go with you."

But she is not calm. A battle drum reverberates in her chest as she precedes Mrs. Davis, ascending the wide staircase leading to her own bedroom, then turning into the hidden landing from which the servants' staircase reaches carpetless into the realm she has rarely before entered. It seems the shushing motion of the sea is following her; she can even taste the salt air. *This is how it will be when I die*, a voice within her declares as she reaches the wobbling floorboards and thin grey carpet of the servants' quarters. *I will start doing eccentric, unpredictable things perhaps in an attempt to distract myself from what is coming. I will start fearing people and things I have never feared before. I will make errors of judgment, and my mind will fly off into tangents, making decisions and acting before I am ready to act.* A rational part of her stands off at a distance, watching her with scientific curiosity, noting all her movements, the way she stands outside Mary's room with its door that hangs open, the way she hesitates, afraid to cross the threshold with Mrs. Davis, worried, at her shoulder.

At last Florence forces herself into the room, reaches the centre and looks around like a terrapin thrown in boiling water. Mrs. Davis hovers just inside the doorway. The dressing table is lodged just beneath the window. The mirror has been removed and is leaning against the wall to the left. A black book is spine up on the surface of the dressing table. Florence considers leaving it. She considers not reaching out to turn the book over. Her arm almost aches in her desire *not* to look at it. But she realizes that, in fact, she must, that it is fate, and that this is the real reason she has come here in the first place. She takes two paces, sighs, reaches out and picks up the book, the pages flopping forlornly between the hard black covers. The pathetic hope that the book might not be what she thinks it is lasts just an instant before the title, *Dracula*, comes into view. An aching pulse shoots up Florence's arm. She pulls the book into her chest and finds herself saying hoarsely: "Start up the fire in the morning room, will you, Mrs. Davis?"

MARY FEELS THE unnatural silence of the house as she polishes the candle holder. She has thrown herself into work voluntarily, not from guilt but from the natural rhythm within her. Since the euphoria of last night, the pendulum has swung into ease and tranquility. Her actions are careful and swift and she has an unfettered desire to be productive and helpful. But just in the last few moments, something unwholesome has seeped into this comfort. Something is not right about the house; an unnatural hush seems to pervade the dust of its hallways since Mrs. Davis was called away, and that silence makes Mary feel rather hopeless and lonely. She tries to shrug off the feeling, working more vigorously at the shine, but the corners of her mouth sink downwards as though pulled by a string, and she finds herself attending more closely to the stillness.

Suddenly, there is a sharp clanging from the wall, a noise so loud in contrast to the hush around it that it at first bears no relation to the ringing of a bell. She looks up to see that she is being summoned to the morning room. She peels off her apron and exits.

THE DOOR IS already half open. Mary glides into the room noiselessly, hoping not to be noticed. Mrs. Stoker sits quite happily, it seems at first, in front of the fire with a black book on her lap. But it is a vision of well-being at odds with itself. For one thing, it does not seem cool enough today for a fire. And there is something asymmetrical both in Mrs. Stoker's smile, and in the fact she should be smiling at all; Mary was bracing herself for a reprimand. And this is quite unlike any expression Mary has seen before; there is something indulgent, mischievous yet vulnerable about it. Her eyes and mouth are in constant movement like someone who is nervous but pretending not to be. Mary looks again at the book, and knows that – whatever Mrs. Stoker's expression – this is its cause.

"Come into the room, Mary," Mrs. Stoker says in a soft voice.

Mary feels her ankle ligaments twitch and ache as she moves into the middle of the room. Mrs. Stoker is silent, watching for a moment.

"Do you remember what I told you about the furniture in your bedroom?" she asks at last.

"Yes, Ma'am," Mary replies, turning her head to one side, trying to see the title. She is puzzled, thinking that the book may not be *Dracula*, after all; Mrs. Stoker would hardly circle around such a subject. She was too much in control for that.

"Well, Mary," Mrs. Stoker asks, "what have you got to say for yourself?" The fluid, uncertain movements of her mistress's expression sink unexpectedly into anger. Mary feels tricked.

"I don't know, Ma'am," she replies.

"You don't know!" Mrs. Stoker raises her voice, half-heartedly it seems.

But a hammer is thumping in Mary's chest, and her body is overtaken by the kind of nerves she has seen in cats before a storm. She knows she can spin in a second into either battle or flight.

"I can't think, Ma'am," Mary blurts, seeing Mrs. Stoker's face getting hotter, pink blotches appearing on her cheeks. It is as though she is looking into a furnace – as though her employer and the fire behind her are one and the same. She cannot imagine a punishment in keeping with this buildup. To be thrown into the street with what money she has – two shillings left – would almost be relief compared to the vague, rising fury she is already facing.

Mrs. Stoker looks down, then holds up the book with an air of triumph. She is gripping one side of the cover; the rest hangs like a battered crow caught by its wing.

Mary sees that this is *Dracula* after all and her respect for Mrs. Stoker's anger drains away involuntarily and with almost magical swiftness. The theatricality is ridiculous. *So I'm reading your late husband's novel*, Mary thinks. *So what? Do you think I stole it from you?* But she realizes that the library stamp is clearly marked on the inside cover, and it's obvious how she came upon it.

"Where did you get this book?" Mrs. Stoker demands.

"From the library, Ma'am," Mary replies, her face burning as much with indignation as with fear.

"Do you know who the author is?" Mrs. Stoker asks quietly, the orange flames dancing behind her.

"Yes, Ma'am," Mary replies, trying hard to keep the contempt from her voice. She makes herself remember how far she is from home, how alien and threatening the city around her might become if she were quite alone.

Mrs. Stoker stares at her angrily for a second. Then her free hand reaches down suddenly and claws the chair leg, gripping hard so that the whites of the knuckles are visible. Pain seems to surge through her face.

Mary is alarmed. She had not considered the chance that the old lady might make herself ill. She suddenly feels guilty and confused.

"Are you all right, Mrs. Stoker?" she asks, bending down slightly, afraid to approach too closely.

"Spying!" Mrs. Stoker hisses.

Mary gives a bewildered smile. "No, Ma'am!" she says as reassuringly as she can.

Mrs. Stoker is breathing hard. Her hand has released the chair leg and she seems no longer in physical distress. Mary begins to feel sorry for her. Suddenly she is just an old woman – her own mother in ten years perhaps.

Mrs. Stoker holds up the book again. *Does she want me to take it?* A pleading look takes over Mrs. Stoker's face. Mary reaches halfway towards the book. Mrs. Stoker does not move it away at first, but then does very slightly, lodging the cover awkwardly between her palm and wrist.

There is a second of uneasy intimacy as their eyes lock at close quarters. Fear spills from Mrs. Stoker's pale eyes; pity oozes from Mary's. The emotions meet with such vivid force and mutual realization that both of them instantly know their relationship is changed forever. The notion of Mrs. Stoker's superiority, upon which all the old lady's comfort rests, will no longer be able to sustain itself.

Mrs. Stoker lurches backwards in her chair, pursing her lips, picking up the broken driftwood of her former composure. "Mary," she says at last, her breathing more steady. "Open the fireguard."

Mary walks silently around her mistress. She picks up the long, brass guard-handle standing by the hearth and, with it, clinks open the guard. Mrs. Stoker turns halfway towards Mary and the fire and holds the book suspended.

"Put it in and close it," she says weakly, turning her face entirely from Mary as the weight of the book leaves her hand. Mary now holds the book. Without a word, or even much hesitation, she finds herself following her mistress's instructions. The book lands closed, hitting the coals with an uneven thud. Sparks waver upwards and the fire makes a few tentative licks around the cover. A sizzle follows, weak and anticlimactic. Mary stands watching for a moment as the fire wobbles and ducks, reluctant to set about the task of devouring its dense subject. Then she closes the fireguard. *Is it inevitability that makes me follow her instructions so obediently?* she wonders.

Is it fear of hunger and unemployment? She is amazed to realize it is neither of these things. It is rather that she has looked into the vast canyon of Mrs. Stoker's desperation and sadness and has found herself dwarfed. She has seen a whole lifetime of unhappiness, dread and disappointment, and a corresponding span of hope, desire and love. Mary is suddenly afraid of the next forty years and she is humbled by the feelings of one who has already lived them.

AFTER MARY GOES back to her work, Florence is left alone. The house is silent now. Like a war zone after bombardment, every flicker and squeak of life has moved to some far-off place. Even the parrot is still. A numb unreality hums in Florence's ears.

A few moments ago, Mrs. Davis entered and asked if she needed anything. She spoke nervously, as though she knew all about the disorientation, about the way she keeps acting strangely and can't seem to stop. *A laughingstock with my own servants!* Florence tells herself cruelly, wanting to wound herself, needing to create a sharp, bleeding gash where pain stubbornly refuses to rise.

Florence dimly understands that in reality no one sees her as a laughingstock; that, if anything, they pity her. Even the little uneducated girl from an obscure village in her home country, pities *her*, the widow of Bram Stoker, barrister and author. But she does not let this thought linger. It is much harder to face. It gives her no enemy to rage against, no focus for her unhappiness. And she needs an enemy, even if it is only herself.

She has no idea, none at all, why she went so far as to burn *Dracula* in front of her maid and make herself seem so thoroughly deranged. It was an impulse, a fear swung wildly out of control, like a misdemeanour which grows into awesome and terrifying proportions as the culprit commits greater and greater crimes in the process of concealment.

The idea started when she asked Mrs. Davis to light the fire. An image flashed in her mind of her husband's book burning on it. *Is that why I asked Mrs. Davis to light the fire?* And there was satisfaction and relief in the picture. Because she *could* burn the book if she wanted to, it gave her a little thrill of power. She could cause terror and confusion to rise in another as well as herself, and she knew this would be a welcome distraction. But it was not a plan. It all happened by accident, like a landslide. She dared herself and found herself following the dare like a sleepwalker. She wanted to engage the army of devouring ants in open battle, and in doing so she had given them all her power. She had *turned* them into monster insects with yard-long pincers of steel. She had given that army the power to overthrow her. Perhaps she was tired of waiting, tired of the invisible legions approaching inch by inch.

And her follies were not over; she had no idea how long it might last. A moment ago, when Mrs. Davis had asked her if she was all right, she had said – and again she has no idea why – she was "seriously considering Mary's future here." It was like a voice running through her, drawing words up from some primal well of self-destruction. And those words had trapped her even more decisively. Now it was a matter of pride. She had made an issue of every foolish thing she had already done, and she had committed herself to more. She was a boulder rolling downhill at an ever-increasing rate. Now she would *have* to dismiss Mary from her service to save face.

FLORENCE FEELS THE past rising around her. Through the unnatural silence she hears the banging of carpenters' hammers, the stomping up and down corridors, the bellowing of minor players. She is willing the present away from her, drawing on whatever shadows will disperse the unnatural, claustrophobic silence. She is walking along a passageway somewhere in the bare honeycomb of tunnels, wardrobes, and scene docks that make up the Lyceum backstage. Mothballs, turpentine, and wood dust mingle in the dim air. Suddenly, from a doorway to the side a head like Punch, ghastly, painted and aged beneath the offensive brightness, pokes itself into the corridor, stares at her blankly, and then disappears again. One of the imps from *Faust*, Florence thinks, shivering. There is spontaneous laughter from a closed dressing room door as she walks past, turning right into the corridor of the lead actors.

"William!" she shouts with a sense of ownership. She knows that Irving does not tolerate interruptions this close to a performance, but she resents the fact that her young son is swallowed up somewhere in the bowels of Irving's theatre. She feels as though he has been taken from her, corrupted by the customs of theatrical life.

Suddenly, another goblin appears, this time scampering out of Irving's dressing room at the very end of the passageway. It is a child this time, not a man, his face painted with the visage of the devil: black eyebrows, a folk beard, black under his eyes. It is William. A wave of anger rises through her. She feels as though her own role has been usurped, her son tricked away from her by this make-believe life that swamps their family. A panic comes across her that William will grow up like her husband.

She makes an exasperated noise as her son runs up to her, excited. She bends down and starts trying to wipe the paint off with a handkerchief. William stands before her laughing but flinching from the blows from the handkerchief, wanting her to join in the joke.

"William!" she says loudly so that Irving might hear from his partly open door. "What have you done to yourself?"

"It wasn't me, Mother, it was Mr. Irving," William says innocently.

"Well, that was very silly of Mr. Irving," Florence replies, still working at the greasepaint which is only smudging and looking worse.

"You must pardon me my folly, my dear Mrs. Stoker," Irving's voice booms out from beyond the open door. "Lucifer was, after all, a fallen angel and the lad has the look of an angel about him."

Florence glances towards the open crack in the door. She feels herself half invited by the voice into this forbidden place and she knows she may never have such a chance again.

"Go and find your father, William," she says quietly. "I need to speak to Mr. Irving."

William runs off instantly and happily with his absurdly smudged devil face. Florence walks towards the half-opened door and knocks.

"Come!" shouts Irving.

Florence crosses the threshold, feeling some trepidation. Irving is alone. He is gazing into the mirror, draped from head to foot in a one-piece suit of scarlet. The hood is down for a moment and he is still applying greasepaint to his face, thickening the black eyebrows, turning himself into the image of Mephistopheles.

Florence pushes the door behind her so it almost closes.

"The perfect devil," she says, surprised at her daring.

Irving turns around. "Thank you!" he says proudly. Then he looks back towards the mirror and resumes work upon his face.

Florence feels as though she is trespassing. The strong smell of the greasepaint and the other perfumes of Irving's profession – eau de cologne, leather polish, vinegar – mix into the austere atmosphere. There is no carpet beneath her shoes, just wooden boards. The dressing table and mirror, a rouge chaise longue and a Japanese-style screen are the only furnishings, and they are spaced far apart. It is a frightening, alien bareness which surrounds her. It tells of feelings exposed, taboos ignored – the opposite of the plushness that surrounds her own life. She wonders at a man who can walk out in front of many hundreds baring his soul as Irving does.

Florence circles around the edges of the dressing room, approaching slowly. She feels she must say something quickly. The longer her presence is unexplained, the worse the silence will be when he turns to find she is not gone. Florence draws near to his left shoulder like one edging along a tightrope.

"William is like his father," she finds herself saying softly. "He is sensitive, easily influenced, reluctant to put himself forward." There is a hint of accusation creeping into her voice now.

She sees Irving's eyes flicker in the mirror as he paints his left eyebrow to a sharper point. He would like to gauge her expression without looking directly at her, she thinks, but she is not in the reflection.

"We both understand Bram," he says nonchalantly.

"*I* understand Bram," she says in a proprietorial tone. Then she relents slightly.

"I'm just not sure," she begins gently, then comes to a pause. "I'm just not sure," she repeats and looks childlike towards the bare floorboards. "I'm not sure that I understand ... you." The words have trickled out at last like spilled wine. She gasps. This is far too close to intimacy, she thinks, and the false propinquity is cloying. She is angry with herself, with the way she has misrepresented her feelings. Worst of all, she is angry that she has put the actor centre stage yet again, despite her resentment that this is where he always dwells in her life.

Irving's face is slowly turning towards her. "My dear," he replies, ease and gratification showing behind his Satan mask, "there is nothing to understand."

Florence takes a deep breath. This time she determines to be practical and precise. "Mr. Irving," she says, pressing herself backwards into the wall, "why did you hire another writer to adapt *Faust* for the stage and not simply give my husband the job?" Her heart is beating like a mallet but this feeling of confrontation is more wholesome than what went on before.

Irving appears to scrutinize her. Florence thinks she can trace a hint of fear somewhere beneath the moist, coloured surface of his skin – perhaps a furrow that is real beneath the painted ones. "Has Bram ever expressed dissatisfaction to you on this matter?" He asks the question, holding her stare for a moment, then turns once more to the mirror. There is no trace of sarcasm or doubt in his voice; it is formal and respectful in tone. But Florence knows that he must know the answer. Already she finds herself shrinking.

"No," she replies honestly. She thinks of leaving, grateful that nothing awful has happened, no argument or recrimination that might find its way to Bram. Then she remembers the feelings that have brought her here; she tries to stir them into action, knowing she will regret this opportunity if it slips away. "But you know how important writing is to him," she says. "You know how desperate he is to make his mark."

Irving is refining the lines on his brow. Other than the movement of his wrist, he is motionless and silent. His poise is unbearable.

"Do you think there is anything I do not understand about your husband, Florence?" he asks in a voice gentle and open, not boastful or insolent as the words might suggest. Florence wants Irving to sound rude and overbearing. She is frustrated that he does not.

"If you understand," Florence asks, sagging against the wall, "why don't you help?"

"With any talent and any venture, my dear Florence, ripeness is all." Florence feels her stomach jump slightly at the style of address – so warm and intimate – but also with its closeness to her husband's poetic, metered way of talking. She has rarely heard Irving speak so fluently or to slide out quotations that synchronize so well with his meaning. "Until success falls naturally upon Bram's shoulders," he continues, "until it scatters down upon him like autumn leaves, then he must merely share in the glory of the Lyceum."

"*Your* glory," says Florence cynically.

"*Our* glory," corrects Irving. Then he turns around and looks at her intently. Florence finds it ridiculous, the devil's face with such a serious expression. But it *is* serious, serious to the point of earnestness. His unwavering dark irises fix her like righteous bullets. "If you think I do not praise your husband enough Florence, it is because that would be like praising myself."

You've never found any difficulty in doing that, thinks Florence, but she only smiles sadly. She thinks of the man before her as a clown, albeit a successful and brilliant one. She is reflecting on how inextricably her husband's fate is bound to him.

"We are demi-spheres, Bram and I," Irving continues, returning to his face in the mirror. "Our fates are joined." Florence watches, almost past caring now, wondering what poem or melodrama he will plunder next for his extravagant claims of friendship. He is using her to warm up, she realizes. He is airing out his lungs for the performance. "Do you understand, Florence?" he adds, strengthening the white between the furrows on his forehead.

Florence leans back against the wall, relaxed now, surprised he has given her another chance to assert herself. "No, not at all," she says matter-of-factly. "Not even slightly."

"We are part of the same whole."

Florence lets out an unhappy laugh. "Well," she says, her eyes narrowing, "that makes me feel very left out." Immediately, she wishes she had not spoken. Something private has been revealed. It is Irving's hypnotic mix of gentleness and insolence that has woven it out from her; his undulating interchange between style and content.

Irving looks towards her again. "But Florence, you are the very jewel of our lives," he says, leaning towards her affectionately.

"*Our lives?*" Florence repeats, her face burning as she wishes he would remember who he is.

"No one could be more important to us," he adds, replacing the brush in the can and turning towards her once more.

"Us?" she repeats, hoping he will reverse his mistake quickly. She finds it disorienting, like thunder on a clear day. She wishes she could believe he was being malicious. She would better know how to deal with it. But his sincerity is overwhelming. It is as though she has been enveloped in Irving's world of fantasy and distortion. And the terror of it is that here the distortions seem real, normal and decent; they are allied to politeness and respect.

"Us," Irving repeats firmly.

She stares at him. The silence lengthens. Florence feels her lip droop and quiver slightly and she envies him his armour of paint. She tells herself he would not be so brave or bold without it.

"Us?" she says again, tugging at his supreme presumption, unable to leave it alone.

"Us," he repeats again, his voice full of understanding and deliberation, with the certainty of truthfulness. Something beyond Florence's understanding has reached inside her world, something dark and unwholesome, something which merges the barriers and borderlines upon which she relies for her balance and sanity.

And then it happens; a storm breaks within Florence. Her sinews and nerves take on a life of their own, propelling her along the bare floorboards towards the door. Solid walls have for the moment become a waterfall, an irrational whirl of constant movement.

Before her world stops spinning she is in the corridor outside Irving's dressing room. Tears have spilled onto her cheeks and she is leaning up against the wall, her chest heaving.

CHAPTER IX

The leaves scatter and swirl, following William down the street, or so it seems. The very atmosphere is pulsating with life, whispering with triple-echo softness through gratings and up servants' staircases. The breeze passes him, circles, turns unexpectedly and strokes his face in passing. The soft hands seem like envoys of a long-dead master, pulling him toward memory; towards the overpowering smell of grease-paint and the cloistered world of the Lyceum backstage. William's face is held rigid by Mr. Irving's dark hypnotic stare and his child's sense of momentousness as the actor continues to paint Mephistophelian highlights into his features. To be paid such attention to by the great one, the man whom even his father – who is standing off and nodding indulgently – defers, is the very crown of his life so far. As Mr. Irving's brush works over his forehead with the black paint, William feels as though he is being initiated, handed over from his father to the master to be groomed and taught at a higher level. He feels a thrill of excitement at the thought. He feels that the great Mr. Irving might be his father now.

WILLIAM TURNS NORTH toward Belgravia, wondering at this ancient, buried desire to be Irving's disciple, and even his son. He thinks of how this plough of memory should turn over such fresh-feeling guilt after all this time. Yes, as a child he too had adored Irving, he finally realizes, just as his father had done; he had longed for the actor's attention and coveted his guardianship. Is this the warp in his manhood that has plagued him all along? Was he stuck between fathers, and did he lose himself in the battle at some crucial stage?

As the breeze shifts over on his face once more, he thinks of all those dreams of youth; the visions of glories yet untasted, valour yet untried. He feels the greasepaint on his face once more and senses a cruel and goading spirit within him. *What drab and unheroic mission are you on at this moment?* the voice asks him.

Maud, as it turns out, agreed wholeheartedly that he should arrange a larger monthly stipend to his mother to cover a payment for Mary. His wife was quite animated at his idea, feeling, no doubt, this was a sign of something stirring in her husband – a sense of mission, perhaps. Maud's trust weighs on him now and he feels himself a sad and parasitic creature, planning and conniving beyond the scope of any decent woman's imagination. If only he could release that part of himself that wanted to exploit the situation and let it tumble into its dim animal cave, leaving the noble part of himself alone. How righteous he would feel, then, how like the knight of his childhood imagination.

He thinks of the unspeakable creature within him and wonders for a second at all the things that might happen if he lets this animal have full sway and act out his darkest desires. He imagines his unclean hands reaching out in the darkness, waiting to fall on vulnerable flesh. And as the vague form of the victim turns into Mary, the boulder of unease turns in his chest. She has become suddenly younger in his mind; she is no longer connected with the Ritz and tea nor with their mild flirtations in his mother's home. She has become connected rather with his boyhood, with his young self in Irving's dressing room. He finds he cannot mature her into a woman in his imagination even for a moment. She, like him, appears as a trusting one amidst overbearing giants. And her trust now destroys his passion. He lets the dark fantasy loose and, with a shiver, presses on in the direction of his mother's house, afternoon fog descending around his shoulders.

THE WALLS DRIP with a steady hollow ring – droplets hitting an unseen basin. Florence tries to block her ears to the sound but she feels paralyzed. A group of men – she knows Bram and Irving to be among them – are murmuring something beyond her vision, somewhere by her feet. Florence's gaze is fixed at the ceiling of the vault which throbs at intervals, its sparse deep red veins bloating, illuminating the dark capillaries around them and then fading back into the stone.

The mumbling men have decided something. Bram's face appears, smiling but a little worried beneath the beard. He looks a little old today, his shoulders hunched. He carries a thick wooden stake sharpened roughly to a point, but carefully varnished even on the most jagged parts. Irving, all in black like a priest, stands off holding a black book, mouthing the words as if trying to memorize them before a performance.

"Don't worry, Florrie," Bram says to her softly, "it's just a rehearsal."

"What do you want me to do?" Florence finds herself asking.

Bram sighs and draws a little closer to her ear. "Well confidentially, this is not very good," he says. "It's a foreign play. They've made a muddle of the thing. But we have to perform it anyway."

He rests the stake on her chest so that the point nips the skin between her ribs. A small piece of stone from the ceiling of the vault lands on her forehead; it is soggy and warm.

"The theatre's on fire!" shouts Irving, looking around at the dropping wet clay. There is still no audience, just her grown son, William, who sits dirty-faced and urchin-clad in a dim corner eating a potato, chimney-sweep apparatus at his side. There is no sign of fire. But Irving and Florence's husband scamper rather comically off through a tunnel in the vault, her husband carrying the stake and mallet with him. William watches after them and takes another bite of his potato. More stone falls, landing in dollops all around the crater floor of the cave. Florence pulls herself up only to find she is chained tight to a concrete slab. The links scrape hard against her wrists and ankles. William gets up slowly, wipes himself down and – without picking up his rods and brushes – leaves.

Harder rocks fall and a noise like thunder begins to grow. Florence cannot seem to tell where the sound is coming from;

it seems to be everywhere, echoing and getting louder. Suddenly, there is a crashing sound and white foam gushes from the same tunnel that Irving, Bram and William left through, hitting the floor and spurting up in a thousand bubbles. The sea water first blinds and then drenches her, pulling her hard in every direction, tearing at the manacled flesh of her wrist, stinging her eyes and shooting up her nose. And a moment later everything is calm. She is no longer chained and horizontal, but propped on a cushion. The taste of salt is still on her tongue, but otherwise she is in her own morning room, warmth and silence surrounding her.

She looks at the windows to see fog has descended, the first in a long time. It curls like smoke in places and hangs thick, like milk, edging the dark leaves near the window. Florence slowly recalls her defeat that morning; she disentangles it from her nightmare with an almost callous precision. She wishes to outface the dragon of that humiliation.

Florence runs through the details of her encounter with Mary, feeling the pain yet relishing the chance to face it down. *So this is what happened* – she thinks – *this is what you have brought me to.* Her accusation is addressed to the universe – to everything and nothing at once. She finds her mountain of defiance growing, roving in search of another such battle, one that will sear her with the same hot flames of self-reproach, one that will crack the shell of her anger and spill it into total, outright war.

She remembers the moving picture. She had secured the address at which it was to be shown this evening from Mr. Thring, saying she should know in case she decided to engage her own lawyer. She had no intention of engaging a lawyer when she said this, and did not quite know why she had suggested that she might. But like everything else today, self-knowledge of her motivations descends after the event. An impending battle now stirs in her chest. She was merely thinking ahead, she realizes. She was reserving an option to go forth and meet her enemy.

WILLIAM STANDS STILL at the corner, wondering whether to follow the man who has just passed him. There is a strange, tickling sensation in his chest and stomach, nothing like the fear he thought he would feel. The moment is replaying itself over and over, though the footsteps have died.

He heard the man approach, saw the dark outline of the bowler hat and the shoulders beneath. A middle-aged form with a beard emerged from the fog, an ordinary man with no hint of ectoplasm, no deathly pallor. And the commonplace, unremarkable feeling of it all could almost cause William to ignore one clear fact: the man was his father.

He recognized the style of dress, the beard, even his father's age – in his early forties, six or seven years before *Dracula*. The gait was so precisely as William remembers it, at once brisk, yet with a slight stoop on his left side.

And William carried on walking, for a few moments at least. He carried on walking because he couldn't think of what else he should do. And now he has stopped, realizing the impossible really has come true and that he may as well acknowledge it. His father's ghost has just passed him. He finds himself smiling at the glibness of it all. This is not how a ghost is supposed to appear, he thinks. He merely passed as another man on the street passes, appearing conscious of the stranger, William, acknowledging him with a slight, nervous change of expression, but not looking directly at him or speaking. Such is the custom between men who have not been introduced. William almost missed the incident completely.

And now that his father has appeared to him a second time, William feels a surge of curiosity. *Can I run after and overtake him?* William asks himself. *Does he know he is a ghost? Would he stop and talk and admit the impossible?* But with each galloping thought, he knows the chances of finding the ghost are slipping away. Both times he has seen his father it has been a fleeting moment, one that scoops into his world from nowhere, making little sense if one is to believe in ghosts as messengers. If his father had wanted to speak to him, then why has he not done so? Why appear through glass in the middle of the garden past midnight, or emerge in the fog when appearance is assured to be followed by disappearance? There is an insulating wall between them, William feels. A strong instinct tells him that it means to remain. His father appears just long enough to rearrange the strands of his thoughts. The contact is just close enough to nudge his heart and brain into frantic activity and to question everything he has taken for granted. William knows this alone is a strong argument for disbelief; he knows that it proves his father's image is sent forth not from heaven or hell but from his own unsatisfied, questioning mind. But that does not stop the tingle of pleasure, or the sense of the extraordinary.

William begins walking again slowly, reluctant to leave the site but aware of the futility of remaining. In a short while he turns into his mother's street which is becoming alive with the first signs of Saturday evening activity. A car zooms past, its headlights like twin moons in the fog. Travelling laughter echoes down the canyon of the street. Farther down towards his mother's house, he sees the dark-hood outline of a taxi cab. A figure – his mother, William thinks – emerges from the pathway and is guided in by the waiting driver who then turns and climbs into the driver's seat. William thinks of striding to try and catch the car before it leaves, but holds himself back. The car pulls out and passes him. He presses on, realizing that his mother was only half of his unfinished business.

THE FOG PRESSES thick against the windows as Florence's taxi zooms along. The silence of the journey is unnatural and threatening. She should have brought Mrs. Davis, she thinks to herself, at least for the outward journey. She has so seldom travelled on her own. The nearest she ever came was travelling with William when he was a child and when Bram was busy on one of the Lyceum's American tours. Sadness tugs her heart. What ever happened to that dear little boy? So trusting and open. She remembers the rescue off the coast of northern France when their ship went down; she can see him in front of her again in his sailor suit, wedged fast between adult passengers, so brave and quiet, as the sea spat its salty foam at them in through the swaying blackness.

Then she remembers how he had been snatched and replaced during one of his school terms. The surly child that returned one winter was clearly an imposter. Yet it is he she now has to rely on in her old age. How chivalrous the real William would have been! How dutiful and attentive! She thinks of how she would have thrilled at the glimpses of adventure he would have given her, the descriptions of battles fought, great events attended, palaces and factories built. He would have taken her arm under his and shown her all from a safe distance the way Bram used to.

Florence gazes into the fog and tries to imagine *her* London flying past, the London of confidence, order and lavish gaiety: Oscar with his yellow silk gloves and hair like raven's wings; Irving and her husband with their wild schemes of taking America; the unashamed luxury of the Lyceum with its peacock wing patterns papering the foyer. She thinks of William Gilbert with his magical catacomb sense of humor and his private menagerie of exotic animals. She remembers the little Madagascar monkey he presented to her and how the gift seemed to represent something so touching, as though he had chipped off a piece of himself for her, recognizing a kindred spirit.

Florence stares into the milky greyness wondering about that gift, remembering the tiny clutching hands as the little animal stood on her shoulder. The memory merges into the star in the eye of her portrait which stands on her bedroom dresser. There was such humour and optimism in that drawing too. Was this merely the flattery of a paid artist, or was there really something different about her then? It all feels as distant to her now as ancient Egypt must seem to the crumbling bones and bandages in the British Museum. The car slows to a halt by the curb. The lights of the nearest building blur through the fog, sending a little wave of trepidation through Florence's heart. *Am I really going to go into battle tonight?* she asks herself as she leans forward to pay the driver. *Have I really left hearth and home for the dank uncertainties of this alien territory and unknown foes?*

The driver opens the door for her at last and Florence steps onto the cold ringing pavement. She feels the indifference of the man like tiny icicles in her bones as he zooms off into the darkening fog. She looks up at the Methodist-plain block building before her. She finds it hard to believe that this is where her enemies are hiding. Bland yellow squares of light puncture the greyness all around her, one below, one above.

She forces herself to move without thinking, pushing the heavy painted door which is wedged slightly open. The dust of a low-grade government office or public library pervades her senses in the austere hallway. She can well imagine Bolshevik rumblings echoing around this unwholesome space with its grey, white and black floor tiles and its wide featureless stairway and bannisters leading up. She obeys a neat chalk-written message and arrow on a small sandwich board and begins to ascend the wide stairway. Loneliness reverberates in her heart with each accompanying step. As she reaches the top of the staircase and glimpses the rows of cheap wooden chairs through the open double doors, she feels an unbearable greyness descending. Her face burns as she crosses the threshold avoiding the glances of several curious, drab intellectuals, some young, some her son's age. To her alarm, one of the men, who walks with a harassed air between the screen and the projector, screwdriver in hand, even looks a little like William – round-shouldered and glum-faced. It's as though they could both be part of the same tribe of such creatures.

Florence takes a seat, scanning the others who number fourteen or fifteen in all. She is clearly the oldest here. But she is pleased to see she is not the only single woman. There are two others who appear neither to be accompanied, nor to be together, although they do seem startlingly similar to each other, both about Maud's age but dressed like librarians in deliberately unflattering brown and grey.

The man with the screwdriver now shuffles his feet. He coughs and the sparse audience ceases to murmur. "Good evening," he says, the screwdriver still in his hand. "Some new faces today, I believe," he adds, squinting, Florence feels, in her direction. She feels her blood race again in fear of discovery, but no one looks around. "The film we are lucky enough to have acquired for this evening is a rather remark-able one, reflecting the exciting new movements in German art and the way it translates into the medium of film." The man shuffles, full of nervous twitchings and awkward enthusiasm. Florence is disappointed that her enemies should remain hidden beneath such bland and human exteriors. His gentle-ness is confounding her. "It's a small-scale production, partic-ularly when compared to the very large filmmaking on America's west coast. But that is not necessarily to its detri-ment. The subject of this film," he pauses looking for the right words, and Florence feels her chest hammering in anticipation of what he is going to say about her husband, "is perhaps a surprising one. Um ... the filmmakers have chosen a rather old-fashioned Gothic relic, one that might have seemed to be out of date in terms of style even when it was written twenty-five years ago. But they have turned it into something remarkable."

A flash of violence runs through Florence. She feels her sinews tighten and her breathing turn to short gasps. This is worse than anything. Not only are these people failing to be outraged at the plunder of her husband's work, they are actually lauding the vandals and disparaging the rightful owner! She comes to the very brink of shouting out and interrupting him. But she is held back for a moment, not by shyness but by some vaguer impotence – by the simple task of finding the right words. There are so many choices, so many valid reasons for urgent protest that she finds herself delayed by the selection. And, as the light goes out and the screen flickers to life, she finds her pounding heart beginning to settle. She finds that the interruption she would have found easy a few moments ago suddenly becomes much harder. Uncertainty and self-consciousness have gripped her. She is watching a performance, and her long acquaintanceship with the theatre has taught her that there is nothing more sacrilegious than upsetting an audience.

THERE IS A happy silence between William and Mary. The morning room clock ticks cozily, its creaking wood acknowledging the ease of the situation. Gloved by this feeling, they have drifted onto the subject of *Dracula* again. Mary is excited by her theory; it is a love story, she has tried to explain. William leans forward, takes a sip of tea and listens. Her freshness charms him and she is gaining in confidence and eloquence.

"Don't you see what I mean?" she says, moving forward in her chair. "It's all about people longing to connect with each other, as though they can't get close enough except by drinking each other's blood and sharing thoughts, and when Mina says that Dracula is the saddest soul of all, it's as though she wants the same thing too."

"I'm sure you're right," William says, warmly taking a sip of tea. "People aren't allowed to love in this country. I'm sure at it's core, *Dracula* is a sad love story."

William has taken himself by surprise. *Not allowed to love.* The phrase repeats in his head. *What did I mean by that?* he asks himself. The phrase came out with such conviction and melancholy, he is afraid he has broken through the barriers of propriety when he was not ready to do so. Mary is looking at him intimately too, as though she believes he is talking about himself. A tingle goes through him, a double charge; half excitement, half fear. He realizes he is within easy reach of the girl's emotions. And now that her face glows under the influence of the hearth, and her skirt hisses gently as she moves, he is intoxicated by the power he apparently wields.

William glances at the fire which glows steadily but sizzles now and again with an unusual amount of ash on the surface. He tries to slow himself down, remembering how he felt before he arrived, about the girl's youth and vulnerability. But it is hard because now she looks older and less helpless. In the evening and the glow of firelight, her skin has taken on an almost voluptuous translucence and her eyes and lips are those of a woman, not a girl.

William moves uneasily in his chair and tries to pin his thoughts down to the original intention of his visit, to his plan to put the financial proposal to his mother. There was something noble about this mission, he tries to tell himself; he should not sully it. But an echo twists darkly at the tail of this thought. *How else might my motivations be viewed?* it mocks.

William catches Mary's sympathetic, smiling face and reaches out for a subject that might distract him.

"Have you finished *Dracula?*" he asks.

Mary's expression drops suddenly. "No," she replies. "I won't be able to finish it now."

"Why not?" asks William confused, thinking he has missed something.

"Mrs. Stoker found out and destroyed it."

"Destroyed what?" He thinks of the film, not understanding. "You mean the book?"

Mary looks at the fire and then at William. William fixes on the piles of ash between and over the coals. He raises himself from the chair and approaches the hearth, his eyes resting on the grey dust and what now shows itself to be scattered, scorched paper. He turns to Mary again.

"She burned your book?"

"She made me put it in the fire."

Her voice is wounded and her eyes glisten with incipient tears. William feels the ghosts of Irving's fingertips on his face, and the smell of greasepaint and turpentine overlay the curious burned fragrance in the room. The two events – book burning and face painting – clang together like great bells announcing a new kind of connection between himself and the girl. There is something in the very substance of both actions that breathes the same fumes. And there is some quality in Mary and in the child he once was that now bleed together in William's mind. He recognizes the fear and hurt in Mary's voice just as if it were once his own. Her age does not matter, nor does her ability to pinpoint the injustice in her accuser's actions; in terms of her ability to defend herself she is a child, and it is the helplessness that seeps through her words.

Rogue and knight begin battling in William's mind again – shields and swords clashing and armoured bodies tumbling. Mary joins him at the hearth unexpectedly and they are both silent. "I'll lend you my copy," William says. "And, don't worry. I'll have a talk with my mother and sort all this out." He feels Mary lean towards him and senses her trust. Suddenly, they are orphans together, viewing the ashes of their home. A new kind of comfort descends upon William. He will inevitably do the right thing. The knight is winning. He may as well make it a willing and resounding victory, not one edged until the last moment with conflict and uncertainty. He gives Mary up in that instant, resolving to help her instead.

THE BOULDER IN William's chest swells and turns as he slopes off down his mother's street. The fog has mixed with factory air, creating an unwholesome cocktail, and the chill has him turning his coat collar upward. He wishes he was home. A vision of Maud at her needlepoint flashes before him. He thinks of the quiet, patient, certain air she has about her, and the way her calm gaze sticks to a purpose. The boulder heaves again and he realizes how closely the two correlate – his yearning unhappiness and thoughts of his wife. An unanswered question returns. "People aren't allowed to love in this country," he said to the girl, a sentence quite unbidden and unspoken before that moment. What did he mean by it? He knew right away he did not mean Mary; the words had rolled out with the sadness of some years and from a cave, normally inaccessible, deep within his heart.

William sees Maud, her face touched by fire glow as she reads from his father's book, infuriating him. He thinks of the twin barriers of fear and dishonesty that keep his own thoughts from his wife. He visualizes a huge, wrought iron and dusty chest with a secured lock at the front and a chain wrapped around many times, tight enough for its rust to have become moulded into the metal. The phrase repeats in his head, *not allowed to love*, and he realizes he was not talking about a book, society, or forbidden desire he felt for the girl. He now knows he was talking about himself and Maud.

CHAPTER X

The screen is alive with fear – crooked shadows, madness, storm-bound ships and scurrying rats. Florence's plan to disrupt the evening has long since subsided. She is trapped by the studious young people on either side, by the nauseating power of the film, and by her growing shyness. The film's style does hold some threadlike connection with her husband's writing, something beyond plot, an echo of Bram's twisted nightmare imagination.

If she had really considered her plan in advance she would have realized these things were bound to happen, that she would be unable to object or even to leave. Why should I so want to trick myself like this? *she wonders, staring at the flickering image of the ghost ship floating into the harbour, its mast reaching into the grey sky. The answer comes in the scent of ashes and the dull sound of a book hitting the coals, sending snakelike hisses into her room. She realizes that in burning the book she crossed a line, and that her crumpled,*

abject manner while she acted was a sign of the profoundness
of her desecration.

A tinny piano in the corner of the lecture room sounds a
predictable accompaniment, shuddering at moments of fright,
as the creature with the pointed head and long fingernails
now emerges from the ship's hold with a disgusting smile,
rats scampering around his shoulders and spilling onto the
deck. Florence wonders why people would want to submerge
themselves in such degradation. Is real life not horrible
enough? she berates them. Do you have to fill your eyes and
ears with the darkest of fears brought to life?

Then she wonders how much of this accusation is aimed
at the audience and how much at her husband. Florence's
temples burn and numbness descends. She watches with just
a touch of masochism as the vampire and his vermin army
arrive in civilization and spread the plague. She feels that
this is what has happened to her own country. Since Bram
and his generation faded away, Florence and her kind have
been left unprotected – exposed to the ignorance of sweeping
change, to the grasping hands wishing to tear down what
they do not understand, to Mary with her assumptions of
equality that show through her ingenuous face, to the unfa-
miliar which has itself become her enemy, to the battalions of
insects silently gnawing at the foundations of her house.

The vampire creature crawls up a staircase casting a
hunchback shadow on the wall. Sickness swirls around
Florence's head. She feels a growing heat crackling inside her
like a bonfire. The woman lies face up in her bed and the
shadow of the vampire's hand reaches over her breast, closing

violently into a fist over her heart as though wringing the life out of her.

THE WOMAN SCREAMS silently and Florence finds herself mumbling an "excuse me" into the darkness and trying to rise. But something is wrong: the room sways around her, and her hands come into contact with a stranger's hard elbow and then a knee. Wooden chair legs flicker under blue light in front of her eyes and she can smell shoe leather. Florence is vaguely aware of a fuss of whispering around her. A strong hand has grasped her around the arm and furniture is being scraped backwards. In a few moments more, she is sitting on a chair with a semicircle of people around her. The flickering blue light is shocked away by startling yellow. Faces bear down on her from every direction. The nervous red-haired man that reminds her of William is twitching and pulling at his beard, his eyes now edged with worry. He is asking someone if he can get into an office with a telephone. The dowdy women watch Florence intently. One whispers to the other something about not moving her.

"Where do you live?" the taller of the women asks her, leaning forward. The words penetrate Florence's ears slowly as though through cotton wool. The girl is kind, almost motherly as nurses are supposed to be, Florence thinks. She tries to answer and manages to mumble her address on the second attempt. The dowdy woman presses her shoulder and promises, "Don't worry, we'll get you home."

Within seconds, it seems, Florence is in the back of a car, the same woman by her side. *Did I miss something?* Florence wonders. Vague images, like dreams, have passed by her. Was she really carried like Caesar down the stairs, supported at her elbows and at the back of her thighs, worried voices criss-crossing from one side to another? Through the car window she sees the fog has begun to clear, and the passing streetlights show like yellow blotches. The night is shiny and wet. Florence tells her companion that her husband is dead. She says this as though it is something that has just happened and can't think how to correct herself. The woman looks at her sympatheti-cally. She takes Florence's hand for a second and tells her that everything will be all right. Then Florence slips away, beyond the skimming lights and rising mist, away from the ugly film which peels from her imagination like paper in the wind. Floating, she weaves between potted palm trees and oriental flowers, over tables and chairs with white tablecloths, silver cutlery and crystal decanters. Candlelight flickers in the silver and glass, spilling gold like syrup into the joyfully murmuring space. Men shine in black formal evening dress; women glisten and laugh. A turban or sari compliments the harmonious arrangement like a shimmering flower in foliage of luscious green.

AND AT THE side of the banquet, on a long table, she finds her younger self. She merges into this handsome woman who sits three seats down from her husband, craning her neck his way and smiling. The lavish celebration is upon the stage. The auditorium yawns, its sweep of empty seats looking rather like a backdrop. Someone mentions this and the surrounding company agrees. Words spill out with the ease of liquid honey, ideas embraced and passed on by the group with an unusual consciousness of shared emotions. A Union Jack hangs at the back of the stage, overlooking them all with a portrait of the new king at the centre.

A flavour of momentousness hangs in the air; the century is at last turning, a year or two too late. It needed something to happen first. The death of Victoria and the crowning of a new king provided it. Fear, nostalgia and sadness tumble in the great crashing wave of excitement and Florence, her husband, Irving, Ellen, all of them in the great Lyceum band, are at the very centre of it all.

A glass clinks and Bram stands – a handsome, upright man. She listens with gratitude to the hush and the ungrudging attention paid him. She watches his shining grey eyes with their mournful sincerity. With a profound contentment she listens to his softly spoken phrases, witnessing how he seems to describe the very fabric of their shared emotion.

"We, who have appointed ourselves guardians of that divine fountain of wisdom and inspiration that is the theatre," he says with a gentle pause, "whether the sacred duty we have undertaken is with hammer and nails, mathematical spreadsheets, paints and canvas, costumes, or whether we are in the very front lines with the footlights glaring upon grease-painted faces ..." he gazes at his audience fixing them as though through some quiet hypnosis, "all of us understand in some small way the profound joy of service and devotion to a thing far greater than ourselves. All of us feel that vital thrill of being part of a great performance which is the result of many individual parts coming together selflessly."

There is a murmur of approval from the audience. Florence feels the warmth of happiness but then slips away, falling from her seat once more and sinking upon her back. The silver and crystal have faded and she is lying in some dark and nameless place.

The bed jolts beneath her, clanking the headboard. She knows straightaway that her husband is next to her, crying. Her eyes are closed fast, her limbs unmoveable as lead. She knows Bram is long gone and that she cannot break through the wall of time. But this time, while the noise and rocking movement continue to assail her, it all suddenly makes sense; the tears are simply the other side of devotion, a relationship as natural and inevitable as the sky and earth joining at the horizon. It is the cost of love. All devotion has a price – the thorn piercing the scalp, the scourge on the back. The formula is written in the very air. *Why did it ever seem unnatural?* she asks herself in the enclosed blackness. And a new fear burns through her body that she herself has unpaid debts.

A fresh sensation merges with the rocking beneath her. Something wet is pressing itself into her forehead. Her vision returns and she sees a hovering dove descend at intervals, pushing its wet wings onto the skin below her hairline. The dove repeats this movement to the rhythm of her husband's sobs which now begin to fade. Heat rises like glowing coals from within her and through the wavering light, beyond the hovering dove, she sees her husband step out of his portrait and stand over the side of the bed. Through her confusion she scans the lines on his face; they are exactly as they appeared in the painting, except in three dimensions. She knows this cannot be a dream, the details are too precise. She tries to moan out loud that this is the case. She urgently needs to tell Bram she knows he is real. She yearns for an acknowledged connection to weigh against the great columns of sadness. But the words will not form.

A stethoscope appears around his neck. *Has he become a doctor?* Florence asks herself, wondering what else she might have forgotten. Bram reaches out as the dove flies away and touches her forehead with the tips of his fingers. And as she feels the soft flesh against hers, a myriad of golden wavelets begin to wash over her, like the essence of candlelight from the Coronation dinner. She drinks in the soothing waves which seem to taste like syrup-wine.

And in a moment she is running, lifting up her long skirts so they do not drag upon the stairs as she ascends. Above her a wide doorway radiates generous undulating shafts of light. She swoops up quickly and flies through into a handsome, spacious room which is painted white and lemon yellow. A youthful, ruddy Bram in the centre spins to greet her. It has been so long since she has seen him look so dashing, she has to catch her breath for a second.

"These are the rooms I was talking to you about," he says calmly, smiling at her. Now Florence remembers where she is, in their Chelsea home overlooking the Thames.

"Where's the view?" she finds herself demanding. Her voice, like her movements, is almost girlishly young, in a whirl of vibrant excitement. She feels her cheeks burn with the energy.

Bram's grey eyes twinkle amusement. She has forgotten how ardent he once seemed. "Curiously enough, my Florrie," he answers slowly, "from the balcony."

They both rush towards the rippling white-veil curtains hanging Turkish-fashion over the French windows. In a second they are looking over the balcony and upon the rolling, crystal-green water of the Thames in June sunlight. Barges, sailboats, cargo and passenger steamers hardly move, and the panorama of church steeples, rooftops, gardens and smoking turrets seems like a great tapestry.

"Do we dare take it?" Florence gasps the question.

"Florrie," Bram replies in rounded, comforting tones. "We can dare to take the world. Spices from India, tea from China, sugar from Jamaica." He points out the vessels one by one, but Florence follows his words, rather than the information, excited by his confidence, protected by his masculinity. "Florrie, we have arrived," he announces taking her arm. A new thrill runs through Florence. She is under the wing of a great eagle who means to take her through *Arabian Nights* adventures, into palaces of kings and lands of legends. "Before I finish," he continues, "the whole globe will have heard of Henry Irving and the Lyceum."

Florence is speechless for a moment. She gulps and feels the tears spill into her eyes. Something has overcome her – an emotion so strong it cannot be named until it begins to pass. It has come from all directions at once – from within her own thumping heart, from the blue sky and wisps of clouds, from the moving water and from the breeze wafting through her hair, touching the skin of her cheek and neck. Then she knows it. She has just felt the supreme, unassailable power of youth and the infinite possibilities it holds.

"I will never forget this moment," she says hoarsely. And she is aware that she stands on the very pinnacle of her life. She pauses, collects the strands of her emotions and continues more solemnly, realizing that she is etching words upon time that will not be erased. "I will never allow my thoughts to spiral into dullness, or let this feeling desert me even for a week." She feels the gentle pressure of Bram's arm squeezing hers in approval.

"You will be the bride of Lyceum," he says with infinite gentleness and respect. She can feel the vibrations of his voice tingling her arm. "Your happiness will be our genie, our lantern carrying us all through difficult times. We are all in our way serving the same great cause."

Florence feels a new joy rise in her chest, a sensation of duty and mission of which she has only ever read – something that until now had always seemed too elusive, too abstract for her sex. She breathes deeply. "I hereby promise to play my role," she says, smiling at the rolling waters, feeling benign gods in the crystal sunlight and the perpetually changing breeze. "I will never be dull. At this moment, I can never even imagine being sad or growing old." She finds herself laughing and leaning against Bram's strong shoulder. "I don't believe it is even possible."

"For you, my dear Florrie," Bram replies, "I can well believe it is not."

MARY BRINGS THE white cloth down to Mrs. Stoker's forehead again, but this time the old lady pushes it away. Her eyes stare at the ceiling as though transfixed. Mary cannot even imagine how she will survive. The colours of her skin are so unnatural, a kind of purple showing under her eyes. She seems so far from either sleep or ordinary waking. The doctor rattles away his stethoscope at the foot of the bed. Mary listens intently to his hushed tones as he talks to Mrs. Davis. "The temperature is our immediate concern. We must continue with the cool water and hope the fever burns itself out." His quiet, even voice only accentuates alarm; it is obvious there are decades of practice behind his manner. It is there for a reason and the reason is grave.

Mrs. Davis slips out of the room to see the doctor out. If he is going, Mary thinks, it cannot be so serious, surely. But then she looks at Mrs. Stoker's open eyes; they are as sense-less to her surroundings as those of a fish at market. The hope fades. Mary feels that the very foundations of her life are being pulled from under her. She can almost feel the floorboards shake and wobble. It did not occur to her that Mrs. Stoker would die. Twin spears of guilt and fear twist inside her at the thought. *How might I have prevented this?* she thinks. *And what will happen to me now?* She sees herself with her packing case disappearing into the London fog, stray dogs following her progress, a shilling in her purse.

Of course Mr. Stoker will want to help her, and so will Mrs. Davis. But he will be caught up with grief and Mrs. Davis will be in need of help herself. Her own plight will seem less deserving among those with less selfish concerns. Death is too sacred and too precious. They will all be guiding Mrs. Stoker to heaven, touching her off on the silent barge. Mary's worries will tumble to the bottom of the pile.

Suddenly, Mrs. Stoker says something. Half sigh, half gasp, it sounded like "He came back."

"Don't try to speak," Mary says, hearing the tenderness of genuine worry in her voice. But then she jolts back. Mrs. Stoker's hand suddenly grips the material of her blouse around her neck. Her eyes are vividly alive and looking into hers, her pupils small like pinpricks. And then she laughs – not a delirious prelude to death, but a warm, intelligent, controlled laugh with focus. Crow's feet wrinkle in the corners of her eyes and Mary thinks how out of place the scene looks; with this expression, Mrs. Stoker should be in her morning room with her Chinese tea set, not sick in bed gripping her maid's collar.

Mary tries to haul her hand away, but the old lady's fingers continue crumpling her blouse, twisting the material so it chafes under her arm. "I know he came back," she whispers. Instinctively, Mary's own fingers slip around the old lady's grip, trying to find a secret pivot to draw it away without force. Eventually she succeeds, pushing her thumb into the fleshy part of Mrs. Stoker's wrist. The grip eases and Mary guides her hand at last down to her side.

Mrs. Davis bustles into the room and Mary finds her face burning. She wonders if she should have removed Mrs. Stoker's hand the way she did, and then is annoyed that she should be doubting herself. *Have I been so drawn into Mrs. Stoker's world of distinctions that I would let her hand grip onto me forever?*

Mrs. Davis has drawn up close to her and is looking down upon her mistress. Mary senses she is excited. "She looks better," Mrs. Davis gasps close to tears. "Oh, thank goodness the fever is passing." She touches Mary on the back with her palm. Mary feels suddenly guilty that her own relief is not as unselfish.

Everything is too soiled for direct emotion. Mary's fears for her own future, the way she had to remove the old lady's hand – these things have twisted too much unrest in her heart. She watches Mrs. Davis take over the nursing with a fresh cloth and bowl, and she finds herself retreating to the foot of the bed. She feels as though a hundred invisible hands are clawing at her collar trying to push her in directions she does not want to go. She thinks of Mr. William Stoker's sad grey eyes and that sudden admission about not being able to love. In some odd way, those words have become more and more important since. They have radiated in all directions at once – they are here in this very sickroom echoing from the walls; they are weaving in and out of her feelings of guilt at not feeling more sorry for the old lady. "There is too much in the way for love," Mary says to herself, adding to the phrase. "How can you feel for someone who holds your fate in their hands?"

She watches Mrs. Davis stoop over her mistress, dabbing her forehead, caressing her with soft, reassuring words. Mary feels humbled for a moment. Mrs. Davis feels love, she thinks, despite her position. How inferior a creature she must be to need preconditions in order to happily serve another.

Mary takes herself off silently. She creaks up the stairs to her own room treading as carefully as she can, wanting to disappear for the rest of the evening. Entering her refuge, she is surprised to see the chair waiting for her beneath the black square of the window and the dressing table as she left it the previous night, half-dismantled to provide a window desk. Mary feels a bone-deep tiredness as she crosses automatically to repair her wayward action. She lays her hand on the wooden back of the chair and takes one last look into the night which is clearing. Wisps of steam rise vertically above distant rooftops and an azure tint shows beyond the stars which are beginning to pierce the sky.

She tips the chair backwards, preparing to scrape it away from the window. But things are changing. It is as though she has reached a summit without knowing and has begun to descend. The rhythms of her body become more fluid, less strained and she feels lighter. It suddenly occurs to her that she might be wiser than Mrs. Stoker. The idea feels, in a way, unnatural and runs in a counter-stream against all she has ever learned. But it brings with it an awesome responsibility. If Mrs. Stoker's edicts are senseless, if the old woman's vision is clouded by personal fear and griefs, if Mary can see many miles beyond her orders, then Mary would be the profoundest of cowards to follow them. She would be sinning against herself.

Mary reaches out and touches the window so that it squeaks a little more open on its hinges. She feels the dampness of a million dying leaves in the first draft of air, and is humbled by the stories they seem to witness in her mind. The flavour of this breeze is immortal, she feels. It tells of king-doms rising and falling, centuries tumbling past like seasons. She hears the tramp of Roman legions, the snap of the Norman longbow, the crackle of burning churches. The only truth and permanence worth heeding, this heady feeling tells her, is in her own heart. And her own heart tells her the age of uncertainty is over.

She thinks of Mr. Stoker's words again – *not allowed to love in this country* – and she feels suddenly sad and angry for the grey multitudes huddled in the walls beneath her, and for herself too, stuck in an attic staring down at them. She thinks of *Dracula* and the same mournful phrase seems to spin through its pages – through the descriptions of forbidding castles, through the passage of the young man Harker yearning for the vampire woman's bite, through the mad chase eastward to catch the villain who has infected one of their own. Suddenly, it seems like the saddest of love stories; it is a story infused with the simplest and deepest of human wants, that of wanting to merge with another. It is a love story written for the loveless, for people who can relate to that want only through horror and fear.

Mary presses her hand up to the glass, the skin of her palm tingling with the chill as it edges slightly more open. She feels that years have descended on her shoulders in the past day or so and that the remnants of her girlhood are about to leave her. All her tumbling, conflicting emotions have formed unexpectedly into a pattern, now streaming into a single channel. It is a wholesome, exciting feeling; it carries the promise of some life mission at present too dimly defined to name. Clues and details are scattered in the dark city beneath her. Some are words charged with action: liberalism, Bolshevism, pacifism. Some are in faces imbued with meaning: the features of a boy unnaturally aged under a checkered cap, pulling a cart, looking only downwards at the road; the white, twisted features of a young man on crutches, an empty folded trouser leg beneath him. Battered street corner signs claim her allegiance also. She hears the clink of sword and armour: the phrase, "a battle only half won," comes into her imagination under the heading, "Suffragettes!"

She does not yet know for which of these worlds her adventure has been preparing her. But the process of sifting has begun. She looks out at the night and feels the infinity. Her first choice is simple. It is whether she should live; whether she should follow the stream she is on, let it direct her for good or for ill, regardless of punishments, hardships, embarrassments and humiliations. The alternative comes briefly in a single face: Mrs. Stoker's.

Mary leans forward and pushes the window open wide.

FLORENCE WANTS TO say more to Dr. Harcourt as he puts his stethoscope away again. She wants to tell him about her experience, how it went beyond dreaming, how it submerged her in a golden life she had thought to have long ago withered and turned to dust. She wants to tell him that she carries that life in her once more, that it is pulsating and warm and real and that no one can take it away unless she lets them. She wants to tell him that her heart and soul are bulging with gratitude for everything, that she loves the whole of Creation just for being, and that, right now, it is all infused with the same golden light for her, regardless of place or circumstance.

"Thank you for dropping in again, Dr. Harcourt," she merely says weakly. And the instant she hears herself she knows that the euphoria will not last forever and will soon begin sagging like an air balloon. Yet even while this disappointment arrives, her still buoyant optimism propels her into a new promise – that she will never again forget this golden feeling entirely while she lives.

"So where were you, Mrs. Stoker, when this attack came?" Dr. Harcourt says, fastening his bag and then standing up.

"A moving picture, Dr. Harcourt," she replies, pulling the sheets up towards her mouth, feeling a touch of mischief that she should have such a secret.

"Perhaps it was not to your taste," the doctor replies with a hint of impatience. He seems annoyed that she is not more ill.

"Perhaps not," Florence replies quietly.

The doctor leaves.

Florence is alone. The silence is warm and thick around her as though the air itself were a living organism. Bram's features stand out vividly from the portrait to Florence's right. He seems less sombre than usual in the muted light. The pools of silver in the irises are no longer the endemic tears of the wounded. They convey warmth and understated humour. Florence caresses the face with her gaze, adding touches of her own to the fine details – things only she might notice and love enough to want to see recreated – a stubborn permanent pimple above his left cheekbone, a faint scar on his forehead in the groove of a furrow.

Florence feels a profound reconciliation, like the shifting of a great stone into its proper crevice after many years of dislocation. Suddenly, her love seems to extend into infinity, as though it has been released after years by the realignment. She thinks of everyone she has ever known: Bram, Irving, Ellen and the whole Lyceum set. She thinks of people around her now: dear Mrs. Davis, so loyal and understanding; the poor girl, Mary – a good sort really; William and Maud – trudging though life as best they can with some unnatural burdens perhaps.

She feels guilty at the last thought, realizing that she herself is one of William's unnatural burdens. She starts trying to make vague plans about how to disrupt this troubling pattern. But she gets stuck as a different self-reproach mushrooms on top of the first. She looks towards her husband's portrait again, remembering that awe-inspiring friendship between him and Irving. She realizes that the golden light is especially magical and strong in this area; she can visualize a shining halo of light around the two men as they sit together, making plans. She links eyes with the portrait and finds herself mouthing the word, "Sorry."

"CAN WE GO to bed soon?" asks Maud unexpectedly, laying aside her own book. "I'm tired."

William looks up from *Dracula*. He has been scanning the text aimlessly. The lines have long since become blurred and his thoughts have wandered far away to the unanchored waywardness of his own feelings. He has been thinking of how his habitually suffocated state of mind has been worsening even further lately, threatening to explode his life into scandal and chaos. He has been thinking about how close this seemed to come and how fortuitous and unexpected was the cure.

He bounces the volume around in his hand once more as though acknowledging to himself that this was the key; it was *Dracula* that got him to ask the question, *What is wrong with me?*

"Whenever you like," William replies, putting the book down on the coffee table.

Maud sighs and looks at him, not rising. "What did you do at your mother's house?"

"Nothing, I just came home."

"You didn't have another one of your long chats with Mary?"

William meets her gaze straight-on. Neither of them flinches or colours and suddenly it all seems as innocent as it sounds. He realizes how much he appreciates Maud's practicality, her firm anchor and innate self-confidence.

"Not really," he says. "Just five minutes."

"You'll have to go again if you want to make your proposal about helping with finances."

"I know."

William stares at his wife for a moment and thinks of how she has catalogued everything that needs to be done. She is the finger on the pulse, the watcher on the city walls, stoical, hard-working and keenly intelligent. The heaving boulder in his chest shifts once more, this time decisively. He remembers the woman in the street near the Irving statue a couple of days ago, the way the fur against her cheek reminded him of Maud. He remembers the melancholic weight of that moment, the way a thousand nerve endings seemed to wail inside him with the yearning movement.

He leans forward in his seat now, a realization suddenly flooding inside him. Every fractured desire of the past few days, he thinks, every fanciful instinct, is reconcilable to the feelings he has for his own wife. It is as though several blurred images are coming together into one definable picture at last. *We're not allowed to love in this country*, he told the girl, knowing despite the excitement of the moment, behind the illicitness of the thrill, he did not mean her – the girl to whom he was talking.

Maud suppresses a yawn. William watches pensively, waiting his time, wondering what he's going to say. *Am I going to apologize?* he asks himself. *For what? For fancying myself no longer in love? For mistaking another for her?*

Maud has noticed his strange mood, the furrows on his brow, the indecisiveness about his movements. She raises her eyebrows at him, dabbing away a tear of tiredness at the corner of her eye.

"Well," she says, "what else is on your mind?"

William realizes the impossibility of it all. He sinks backwards in his chair again. *She doesn't want to hear it,* he thinks.

"Nothing," he says, then splutters, "just thinking about my father."

"What about your father?" Maud replies, slightly amused, her penetrating gaze seeming to understand something about William – his need to speak and the difficulty of speaking.

"About the way he charged about from place to place." William sighs. He knows he's committed himself and so forces the rest of the message out. "The way he travelled around the country, to America, to Germany, all for the theatre and Irving."

Maud crosses her hands on her lap. "What were you thinking about it?"

William feels impatience rising in his chest. He wants to scream, "I'm trying to tell you that I love you, you silly woman, why can't you take a hint?"

He exhales deeply again, collecting his thoughts. "Just that I'm glad I don't do that."

Maud is watching him closely. William feels a great tide of vulnerability edged with guilt rise and fall within him. *I've never been this shy before,* he thinks to himself, but realizes the reason straightaway. He has never been so desperate or so worried about communicating with Maud before. His heart is beating hard and he wonders what he can see in his wife's subtle, intelligent eyes. A husband who has almost strayed? A man who has pulled himself back from the verge of disaster just in time?

A moment of suspicion passes over Maud's face, a sardonic half-smile well known to William. But it lasts just an instant. In a few moments another expression sweeps it aside, a warm, full-hearted smile, a smile that seems both from an earlier era, and yet is quite untried – trust and hope with understanding of past failure perhaps.

William understands the smile, and finds his heart committing in a way that would not have been possible a week before. There is all the joy of the unexpected in this moment. The boulder has disintegrated, crumbled into dust and is being swept away on the night breeze like a bad dream.

THEY ARE MAKING love in the darkness. The bedclothes sigh and rustle around them as they move. Linen tingles

William's fingertips like static. He wonders how much of his thoughts are known by his wife. There is something momentous in the very quiet, in the rhythm of their breathing; it seems as though communication must be infinite. And she must at least notice it is different this time, he thinks – there is something younger about them both tonight, something freshly discovered in every synchronized movement. They sound different too – more concentrated, more serious, more serene. Even while William's thoughts spin like shuffling playing cards, there is a peacefulness in himself and an honesty toward Maud. He wonders if Maud can tell he is thinking about the Palm Court at the Ritz, about the times they went there before they were married, and how it seemed *theirs*, the way a certain time and place is owned by young lovers – connected to their joined inner lives by a thousand oblique and humourous references. He wonders if Maud would ever guess he had tried to create the exact flavour of that time with a young woman he hardly knew. He wonders if she could guess at the shallowness of his folly, searching for the rich seam of his most ancient love in the dust around his feet. The magic time of his love is returning now, a glimmer of gold through layers of ashes. A whole cumbersome, hideously constructed prison-like fortress is creaking and groaning and giving way to something sparkling and genuine to himself.

CHAPTER XI

The milky remnants of the fog have lifted. Stars appear slowly like distant spears aiming toward the earth. A leaf falls in William's garden, its vessels choked by recent smog and the oncoming cold. It spins on an eddy and touches down upon the lawn. The breeze sighs restlessly, a flavour of regret diverging around the trunk of the old oak and coming together again, re-assessing itself.

The Regret has been floating on the breeze between Belgravia and Chelsea, skimming over the rich dark-green surface of the Thames, gaining focus and momentum. It holds the ice needles of frost yet to descend, and the warmth of the season fully matured. The Regret communicates freely with all around it – the damp stone, the wrought iron spikes and hooks, the scents which carry all information about human contact, feeling and information. The Regret was stung into existence by a woman's anger and pain and by a younger man's burning uncertainty. It tumbled together from distant places where it had long since been happily dispersed. It was called together into wholeness by the pain of its disso-ciated parts. The Regret began to recognize itself slowly – the life it had once represented, and the woman and man whose silent cries now brought it together.

And now the Regret is getting ready to disperse again into the lives of which it was more recently a part. Boulders have shifted into place, misunderstandings realigned. Becoming a man again has been a painful rebirth. The intensity of love and devotion and hope and pain has been like many hoops of burning flame for the Regret who has been learning to call himself Bram once more. Love, he has found, is of all emotions, the least forgiven. Bram had in life one great love, a soulmate whose thoughts and feelings were part of his own. Bram and his love had in life been on a mission – to create the conditions for inspiration, a divine lamp that would burn in the hearts of men and women who partook of it. It had been the noblest quest of all and they had devoted themselves to it entirely. The Regret – Bram – did not know he would submerge his wife and son in the flames of bitterness and anger.

The understanding and joy Bram had once seen in his wife on their balcony overlooking the Thames did not last the intervening years of so many triumphs and frustrations. It became strangled in the creeping limbs of jealousy and suspi-cion.

And for his son, the flame of inspiration had been buffeted in the whirlwind of changing times. Inspiration had changed into something scorching – unjust and humiliating to the boy. It had become unfaithfulness to his mother, ingratitude of a "great one" towards his father. It had become the vicious inequality the world creates between men. William had made an enemy out of inspiration itself and this had poisoned the spirit in him. He had become lost in a quagmire of loathing and self-doubt.

Bram's wife and son were both dying, their souls withering slowly by increments, until the invasion of chance – a foreign motion picture – made them both cry out to the universe in pain. And Bram responded. He floated in the breeze around their homes. He entered into their dreams, conjuring memories and shadows. He stood in William's garden, beckoning, and walked like a living man through the fog, emerging through the clouds in front of his eyes. He stepped out of his portrait in Florence's bedroom and pulled her into the past.

He felt the fear and anger rise and fall like lava in a volcano, altering its nature until the great change like purest alchemy when fury and grief turns to joy, and darkness of the soul turns to gold.

BRAM LINGERS IN his son's garden only for a moment. He remembers the passage in *Dracula* his publisher deleted, the one in which Dracula's castle crumbles into dust when the vampire is slain. He knows that something similar has just happened to his son – a disintegration of unhealthy personal terrors and suffocating thoughts.

Bram returns to his old home, dissolving into the breeze, allowing the filthy London air to blow by and through him, recognizing the squalid atmosphere from so many years before and feeling it rooting him even further to his old life when the profound comfort in the word "home" was interwoven with the scent of dry soot, factory smoke and river effluence. As he descends into Florence's garden he feels the peace of the house vibrating gently through the brick walls. He knows Florence's torment is over. He knows her to be sleeping, her body recovered already from the fever she invoked upon herself. When she wakes, he knows, she will cease to fear catastrophe, and she will no longer punish herself by pulling the rubble of disaster over her thoughts.

Bram stands in the garden looking up. The young woman, Mary, is awake and looking out. She lets her head drop suddenly. Bram realizes that she is writing at her makeshift desk. Part of Irving – with whom Bram's spirit has long since merged – reacts to the young woman. The strand of Irving is excited by her adventurous, defiant spirit. The feeling tingles through the whole spirit – Irving and Bram. This is the face of the new world, Bram feels. Every old story – from Shakespeare to his own – has to crumble into the earth like fertilizer. Each new generation needs to start afresh. Stories diminish with time. It is inevitable. They need to be retold.

Irving agrees, reminding Bram of a conversation, long forgotten, even between themselves.

A scent draws their spirit into the past, evoking the exact hue of candlelight which flickers slightly in the brandy glasses resting on the polished surface. Cigar smoke rises before Irving's face. The actor is drawn and oddly exhausted tonight, Bram notices. And yet, earlier, he recalls with some amazement, his friend had drawn tears of joy and gratitude from the audience. Shylock had been a triumph, a groundbreaking portrayal in a world polluted with anti-Semitism. Irving had given the merchant such dignity and righteousness with his dark eyes and direct honest stare that expectations had been turned on their heads. "I thought Shylock was a villain," someone had even mumbled on his way into the foyer.

And now, as usual, Bram and Irving are alone late at night discussing all manner of human affairs, their conversation like a comet hurtling through the universe of their joint imagination. They talk of the golden spring of inspiration and of tonight's performance. And quite unexpectedly, Irving takes a deep breath and begins talking of a fear he has never mentioned before. His voice is uncertain and his eyes cast down and tired. He describes standing in the wings before his entrance, feeling the audience on the other side, their pensiveness, the hush and shallow breathing. He tells Bram of an invisible, many-headed monster which lurks on the other side of the curtain, stealing the life slowly out of him with the electric buzz of their constant expectation. He tells Bram that no matter how drained he feels night after night, he knows he can never stop. Performance, he says, is his drug and it sustains his spirit, even while it kills him.

Bram relives the conversation. He remembers how it helped to inform the creation of his vampire – a being that survives as we all do upon the blood of others, a creature that moves effortlessly over the borderlines of empathy and antipathy, virtue and vice, love and hate. He knows that this story, like all others, will be degraded and lost. To seek to preserve any part of oneself is the greatest of all follies and a sure route to unhappiness. The best that can be hoped for is communion – to be part of something greater than oneself.

Bram takes one more look at the lit open window and the golden-haired woman who writes at her desk. He and Irving exchange a secret wish for her and then disperse once more into the night.

ACKNOWLEDGEMENTS

Special thanks to Allan Magee who gave important feedback on a conceptual level, to Noel Baker who helped me to hone the themes of the story, to my editor, Ed Kavanagh, and to Elizabeth Miller for her encouragement. Thanks also to Levi Curtis, Jennifer Deyell, Tony Elliot, Mike Goldback, Andre Kocsis, Ed McNamara, Lara MacKinnon, Jody Richardson, Jana Sinyor, Stanley Sparks and Ed Tanasychuk for excellent feedback. I would like to acknowledge everyone at the Canadian Film Centre. Thanks to my publisher Garry Cranford and to Jerry and Margo Cranford. I would especially like to thank my wife, Maura.

ABOUT THE AUTHOR

Paul Butler is the author of the novel *The Surrogate Spirit*, published in 2000, and a graduate of the 2001 Professional Screenwriters' Programme at Norman Jewison's *Canadian Film Centre*. He is presently developing a number of projects in film and TV ranging from features to documentary series. Originally from the U.K., he came to Canada in 1994. In Canada, he has developed curriculum, written literacy textbooks and worked in journalism, teaching and editing. Before emigrating, he taught English as a Second Language in Greece.

AGMV Marquis

MEMBRE DE SCABRINI MEDIA

Québec, Canada
2003